About the author

Monica Li graduated with a Bachelor's Degree in English Literature and Japanese Studies. Fluent in English, Mandarin Chinese and Cantonese, Monica specialises in technology public relations and she has worked in Hong Kong, Singapore and the United States. She grew up listening to her grandparents' stories about China, and always wanted to share some of these stories to encourage other overseas Chinese people to find out about their ancestors and their home towns. She lives in Singapore.

THE DRAGON PHOENIX BRACELET

Monica Li

Book Guild Publishing
Sussex, England

First published in Great Britain in 2014 by
The Book Guild Ltd
The Werks
45 Church Road
Hove, BN3 2BE

Typesetting in Sabon by
Nat-Type, Cheshire

Printed in Great Britain by
CPI Group (UK) Ltd, Croydon, CR0 4YY

A catalogue record for this book is available from
The British Library.

ISBN 978 1 909984 93 6

To my loving husband Stuart and my wonderful daughter Claudia

Prologue

'Ah-ma visited me last night,' June told her mother as she rolled the glutinous rice dough into ball-shaped dumplings for the winter solstice festival. She didn't get any response from her mother, who was either too engrossed preparing the peanut filling or simply ignoring her nonsense talk. Her mother was brought up as a convent girl, but considered herself a free thinker. In other words, she didn't believe in ghosts.

'Mum, why can't you pretend to be interested in what I have to say? You're always complaining that I don't tell you stuff but when I do, you're more interested in the dumplings!' June decided to get her mother's attention by making her feel guilty.

Just as June expected, her mother immediately stopped stirring the ginger syrup and looked up. 'Bao Bao, you know that's not true.'

If there was one thing she would change about herself, it wouldn't be her freckles, her single eyelids or even her boyish chest, but her nickname. Her grandmother named her Ka Bo, which meant treasure of the family, but her non-Cantonese speaking mother called her Bao Bao instead. It was endearing to be called Bao Bao as a toddler, but not at twenty-one.

As June fought the urge to point this out, her mother asked if her grandmother had given her any winning numbers for the lottery. Her mother was not taking her seriously – but at least June had got her attention.

'Ah-ma looked just like she did when she was alive. She was wearing her favourite sumfoo, the one she wore to my graduation … She held my hand and pointed to the sun, except it wasn't the sun. There was a gold orb in the sky formed by a golden dragon and a phoenix playing, chasing each other's tails. It was beautiful.'

'Aiyoh! You have been watching too many Chinese fairytale movies. Don't think too much about the bracelet. That pawn ticket that your grandmother left you is decades old … I doubt the shop's still in business. Even if it is, the bracelet was probably bought by someone years ago.'

June knew in her heart that her mother could well be right. It was a mystery why her grandmother had left her a pawn ticket for a gold bracelet along with the rest of her jewelry when she passed away. June's father didn't know anything about the ticket, which was dated 1945 – or indeed the bracelet itself – but it must have meant something to her grandmother for her to keep the small slip of paper for such a long time.

Her grandmother, Phoenix, was a generous woman but not wealthy. It wasn't too long ago that she told June that she was going to leave her all her jewelry.

'Ka Bo, I may not be around for very long.'

'Don't say that, Ah-ma! You're looking very well.'

'You're my little treasure … Just let me finish what I have to say. I have only saved enough to pay for my coffin and my funeral, so I don't have much to give you except my wedding heirloom. It was given to me by my father, so it's only right that I give it to you and for you to give it to your future daughter.'

As June remembered the conversation, she realised that she had cried so much her grandmother never got a chance to tell her about the pawn ticket.

'I'll find the gold bracelet and bring it home. That would be Ah-ma's wish,' June told her mother. Her mind was made up.

*   *   *

2

June was born and raised in Singapore but had a strong affinity for China, as she grew up listening to her grandmother's stories about her home country. She knew that her grandparents moved to Hong Kong when her father was only three years old and they subsequently migrated to Singapore in the sixties. She always wondered why her grandparents and father never made the trip back, but told herself that one day she would visit her relatives in the Cheng ancestral village and learn more about her background.

Her father had few memories of China and – like her mother – was very practical. He cared a great deal about his family, but saw no point in reminiscing about the past.

Nonetheless, he wrote to his cousin in Hong Kong and asked if he would accompany June to their ancestral village in Guangzhou.

'Ka Bo, you have to keep in mind that China has changed a lot since we left in 1945. You may find that the China you know from your grandmother's stories may be very different to the one you will experience. After we fled to Hong Kong, people on the mainland went through hard times during the labour reform and Cultural Revolution. We lost touch with many of our relatives, including your grandmother's sister, Jade. I'm not sure if there's anyone left in the village who can tell us much about that pawn ticket.'

'I know, Papa. Apart from hunting down the bracelet this will give me a chance to find out about our history, so I can pass the stories on to my own children. Also this year is the handover[1], so I'd rather hold off job-hunting and enjoy the celebrations in Hong Kong. Thanks for being so supportive, this trip really means a lot to me!'

---

[1] Hong Kong was handed over to China in 1997, ending more than 150 years of British rule.

1

Year of the Dragon

The Chinese New Year of 1916 saw the dawn of the Year of the Dragon. The Chinese believe that the Dragon is the strongest of all the twelve zodiac signs and symbolises good fortune and prosperity. The Wong family house was decorated for the festive occasion with narcissus, lucky red paper cuttings and potted mandarin orange trees. This particular New Year celebration was a special one for the Wong family. Apart from the red packets and new clothes, half-sisters Phoenix and Jade looked forward to the hundredth day celebration for their baby brother, which coincided with the first day of Chinese New Year.

Their father was away on business when their brother was born. As Mei's due date drew close, Wong found it hard to concentrate at work. He prayed hard it was a boy. Despite all the sexual potency tonics he was taking, he questioned his virility with age. Since his main wife Ling was barren from a difficult birth of their first born, Phoenix, his hopes were pinned on his second wife. The two women got along like sisters; Wong did not want to disrupt the family dynamics by taking another wife. He still remembered when Ling suggested that he took a concubine.

'I know how badly you want to have a son to inherit the family business and yet I have only given you a daughter. You have been an honorable husband; you have never once said you

5

would take a concubine. Since I cannot bear any more children, it is only right that someone else is able to fulfill that duty.'

'Oh Ling,' he sighed, 'I don't blame you at all. I have to admit that I am not so noble – I have considered taking a second wife. I just didn't know how to bring it up without being insensitive to your feelings. Thank you for being so understanding. You know I will make sure that you are always respected as the main wife.'

Wong had been at home for the births of his two daughters, and had found it hard not to be disappointed on both occasions when the midwife announced that it was a baby girl. A business associate's wife had said that the shape of the mother's stomach was a telltale sign of the baby's gender. He was not one to believe in old wives' tales but if it were true, judging by Mei's pointed belly, he was finally going to have a son.

He was very excited, but not surprised, when he was told that Mei had delivered a boy. As soon as he received the good news, he wrote to Ling.

Dear Wife,
It is truly a blessing that our ancestors have given us a boy at last. Please light a lantern at the ancestral temple to celebrate the birth of our dear son. Do make sure you send someone to guard the lantern day and night. I trust you to take care of the mother and child in my absence, but I will return as soon as I can. Please plan for the hundredth day celebration ... spare no expense.

Ling knew just the person to guard the lantern. It was a common practice for families who wanted a son to steal the lanterns for luck. Their manservant Fatty stole one for the Wong's last year, so it was only logical to send him to protect their own from theft. Fatty (who had lost weight since the family got their own rickshaw), welcomed the temporary reprieve from having to transport the girls and their mothers around town.

Once the lantern was lit, Ling's main priority was taking care of Mei. During the first month, when Mei was confined to her bed to recover from the birth, Ling made sure she was given plenty of nourishing food each day.

'Big Sister, you are so good to me. I cannot thank you enough. I am grateful that you have never treated me less than an equal since I stepped into this household seven years ago.'

'Don't say that. You are family. Why shouldn't I treat you as such? I am just glad that Guan Yin, the goddess of mercy and provider of children, heard my prayers and gave us a son to continue the Wong family name.'

The harmony between Mei and Ling meant that their daughters in turn grew up without any rivalry. Far from being jealous of the attention given to the newborn, Phoenix and Jade were happy to have a new playmate. Instead of cloth dolls, they could now play with the real thing.

On New Year's Eve, both girls stayed up late to bless their parents with longevity. Outside their bedroom they heard the incoherent chatter of relatives exchanging the latest gossip, interjected by the shuffling sound of mahjong tiles. Every now and then, neighbourhood boys let off firecrackers to chase away the Nian, a mythical beast said to devour people on New Year's Eve. With all that excitement, they couldn't have slept even if they'd wanted to.

Phoenix and Jade stayed awake talking about the banquet their father was hosting for friends and family at the ancestral temple in honour of the ancestors who had given him a long-awaited son. Their grandfather was a well-respected village head and their father had made his fortune from a lucrative trading business. Apart from the usual friends and relatives, the girls expected their father's business associates to attend the celebration.

'I will sit on Uncle Lam's lap if he brings us those delicious English butter cookies like he did last year,' said Jade. She was six, a year younger than Phoenix – but precocious. Jade was the more attractive of the two sisters and knew how to use her charms at an early age to get what she wanted.

'I'm looking forward to the show tomorrow! Father gave the opera people a big red packet to perform at the banquet.' Both sisters were Cantonese opera fans who loved to dress up and sing their favourite tunes. Jade knew that opera performers held a very low status in society – but that didn't stop her from dreaming about being the female lead.

'I know why Mother requested them to perform *Journey to the West*. It's based on the legend of the Monkey King and his quest to live forever. This is a lucky story for birthday celebrations,' said Phoenix thoughtfully. 'And it has Guan Yin, a patron goddess of mothers.'

'Ma-ma said that Guan Yin was so moved by Da-ma's devotion that she gave us a little brother. Jie, I will give up meat like Da-ma and pray for a good husband.' Jade referred to Phoenix's mother as Big Mother, 'Da-ma', and Phoenix as sister, 'Jie'.

'I bet you won't last more than a day unless you plan to skip the roast pig tomorrow!' Phoenix laughed. 'Anyway, we better get some sleep so we can get up early to wish Ye-ye and our parents happy New Year.'

'I would very much like to hear you tell the story of the Chinese zodiac signs ...' Jade always enjoyed her sister's bedtime stories and Phoenix gave in easily. 'All right, but promise me you'll sleep after I tell the story!'

'A long, long, time ago, the Jade Emperor summoned all the animals to visit him in the Heavenly Kingdom on New Year's Day. As a reward, he would name a year for the first twelve animals. Mortal beings born in the year of the zodiac sign would share certain characteristics of that animal.

'At that time, the Cat and the Rat were good friends and were as close as kin. Both animals rejoiced when they heard the news and decided to go together. On New Year's Eve, the Cat said to the Rat, "Brother Rat, please wake me up for the ceremony in case I oversleep." "You can count on me. Go ahead and nap. I will call you when it's time to go," the Rat assured the Cat.

'The Cat thanked him and promptly went to bed. But the Rat broke his promise. He woke up very early the next morning and left without the Cat.

'In the lake there lived the Dragon, who also received the command. The Dragon was a magnificent creature with shiny scales, a large nose, and a long, thick beard. He thought to himself, "With my fierce looks, surely the Jade Emperor will choose me!" His only flaw was his baldness. The Dragon decided that a pair of beautiful horns was what he needed to compensate for his bare head.

'Just then, the Rooster strutted by the lake. The Dragon was surprised to see that the Rooster had a pair of horns. "Brother Rooster!" the Dragon shouted excitedly. "I would like to borrow your horns for my visit to the Jade Emperor."

'The Rooster replied, "Sorry, Brother Dragon. I am visiting the Jade Emperor too." "Your horns are too large for your head. How about you lend them to me? I have no hair and have far greater need for a pair of horns like yours," the Dragon pleaded.

'The nosy Centipede, who had overhead the conversation, decided to chip in. "Brother Rooster, if you lend your horns to Brother Dragon, I guarantee you will be rewarded many times over."

'After some consideration, the Rooster decided that he could do without the horns and lent them to the Dragon – with the Centipede as the guarantor.

'When the Ox received the Jade Emperor's invitation, he said to himself, "It's a long journey to visit the Heavenly Kingdom. I'd better get a head start since I move so slowly." The Rat hitched a ride on the Ox's back without him realising. Just as the Ox arrived at the Heavenly Kingdom, the Rat jumped over the Ox's head and became the first to greet the Jade Emperor. The Jade Emperor thus chose the twelve animals as they arrived to be the signs for the years – Rat, Ox, Tiger, Rabbit, Dragon, Snake, Horse, Goat, Monkey, Rooster, Dog and Pig. By the time the Cat woke up, he had missed the ceremony. That is why the Cat and the Rat have been enemies ever since.

'The Rooster never did get his horns back from the Dragon. He took revenge on the Centipede by swallowing him whole. Every morning from then on, the Rooster would call to the Dragon to return his horns.'

And as Phoenix reached the end of the story, Jade was fast asleep.

Phoenix had a hard time sleeping as the New Year's Eve revelry went on all night. She was wide awake when she heard the rooster crow. 'The poor animal is still looking for his horns,' she thought to herself. 'Little does he know he's going to be dinner tonight.' Phoenix had a soft spot for the rooster as she raised it from a chick, but always knew it was going to be slaughtered. She had already saved some of its beautiful feathers to make a shuttlecock as a birthday present for her little sister.

Jade stirred in their bed as the morning sun slowly warmed the room. Phoenix gave her a gentle nudge and said, 'Let's get dressed. Ye-ye will be waiting for us to greet him and he'll give us red packets!' Jade usually woke up late and often got chided for not paying respect to her elders in the mornings, but this morning she was keen to get up and show off her new set of clothes and shoes.

'Jie, can you please help me tie up my hair while I put on my jacket?' Jade asked. She was no longer the baby of the house and looked to Phoenix to help her get ready since the adults were too preoccupied with her baby brother to bother with her. Phoenix obligingly tied Jade's hair in pigtails before she did her own.

Both girls were dressed in their finest when they stepped into the reception hall, where their family gathered for breakfast in the mornings. Phoenix wore a red silk jacket with hand-embroidered plum blossoms, while Jade wore a green silk jacket with butterflies and blooming peonies. As part of their domestic education Phoenix's mother was teaching them how to sew. The girls proudly displayed their colourful hand-sewn shoes, with intricately embroidered lotus flowers that hinted at their mothers' desire to have more sons.

'Ye-ye, happy New Year! We wish you good health and longevity,' Phoenix and Jade greeted their grandfather in unison.

'You're both very obedient. You're big girls now. Be filial to your parents and harmonious with each other.' Elder Wong grinned from ear to ear, bouncing his grandson on his lap as he beckoned the two sisters forward to receive their red packets.

Phoenix and Jade greeted their father and mothers before the family proceeded to the ancestral temple to pay respect to their ancestors.

It was the first time Mei and the baby stepped out of the house. The boy was dressed in a smart green waistcoat, white navel cover, red and green divided trousers and hand-sewn shoes embroidered with tigers to ward off the evil spirits. He had been referred to as 'little one' since he was born. To mark his hundredth day, his grandfather gave him his first name – Choy, the Chinese character for fortune. Choy also received a good luck charm in the shape of a rabbit, his zodiac sign.

Fatty took Wong's wives and the baby to the temple in the rickshaw while the rest of the family walked there. The temple was only a short distance from the house, but it would have taken too long for Ling and Mei to walk with their three-inch 'lotus feet'. Although both his wives had bound feet, Wong could not bear to have his daughters endure the same physical torture. He was confident that the family's status and wealth would attract respectable suitors – regardless of whether the girls had bound feet or not.

On the way to the temple, the streets were lined with red paper from the firecrackers set off the night before. Phoenix made sure her sister didn't run through the litter in case the red paper stained her pretty shoes. She noticed that this morning, unlike other mornings, there was no monotonous incantation of the traditional Confucian classics at the village school. Instead she heard the lion dance troupe performing door to door, playing gongs and drums, to usher in good luck and fortune in return for a red packet.

They lived in a small village of nineteen families, of which most shared common ancestors. The Wongs and Chengs were descended from the early founders who migrated from Shanxi because of internal wars during the Ming Dynasty. The Wong descendants lived at the north end of the village, while the Cheng descendants lived at the south. Each built their own temple to honour their ancestors.

The Wong ancestral temple was busy with worshippers that morning. An exotic smell of burning incense and flowers lingered in the air. The temple was dedicated to the clan's patron deity, Guan Gong, and housed the ancestral tablets of deceased Wongs.

Outside the temple, Fatty pointed out to the girls which lantern he had been guarding for their baby brother, Choy.

'Can you spot our lantern, Misses Wong?'

'Easy, it's the most beautiful one, just like my baby brother,' Jade exclaimed and clapped her hands with glee.

'Be careful what you say about the young master. We don't want evil spirits to be attracted to him,' Fatty reminded the girls.

Once inside the temple, adults and children alike prayed for good health and fortune for themselves and their family members. Wong made a special prayer to his ancestors.

'Thank you for giving me a son to preserve our family name. Please watch over him and keep him safe and strong so he can one day take over our family business. Thank you for our success – please help our family to prosper so we can honour you … our ancestors. I offer up humble gifts for your continued blessings.'

For this special occasion, Wong paid for an extravagant offering of roast pigs, chickens, steamed buns, sweets, paper money and incense. In addition, he gave the temple keeper a red packet to add Choy's name to the genealogy records. Phoenix recalled Jade's vow to abstain from eating meat as she watched her pinch off a tempting piece of the crackling.

Phoenix and Jade kept close to their mothers while they watched other children in the crowded temple. The girls had limited interaction with their neighbours as they were expected to stay at home, while their brother would go to school when he was old enough. They didn't need to do household chores like girls in poor families but they had to learn how to cook and sew – essential skills for a good wife.

'Jie, don't you think our family looks elegant in our silks compared to the villagers dressed in their plain cotton?' Jade remarked.

'Remember what Ba-ba said about being humble – and it's New Year, we shouldn't say bad things about other people!' Phoenix admonished her sister in a hushed tone.

Phoenix felt self-conscious that she was dressed so well and stared at her feet when she caught other children looking at her. She turned her attention to the genealogy book as the temple keeper wrote down Choy's name in Chinese calligraphy.

'Ma-ma, why are our names not in the book?'

'You are a silly girl! Only male descendants are recorded in the book and receive money every year from the ancestral estate. When you get married, your name will be added to your husband's genealogy,' her mother explained.

Phoenix looked at Choy and realised why it was so important to her parents to have a son. Her father was her grandfather's only surviving son. Her two uncles had married but died young, without any children. If her father were unable to produce a male heir, the family tree would end with her father with no one left to worship their ancestors in the spirit world. As the eldest son, Choy now held that responsibility.

'Don't look so glum, Phoenix. We won't marry you off too quickly but when we do, we'll find you a good match.' Her mother thought she was afraid of being a wife. 'The lion dance troupe is here. Go join your sister outside – we'll be out soon.'

Before Phoenix left the temple to look for her sister, she offered a special prayer to Guan Yin to give her a baby boy, so she could make a good wife when it was her time.

It was a long day for the girls. After the temple visit, they went home to wait for visitors to arrive. Since Elder Wong was the village head and patriarch of the family, many people came by to pay their respects to them before visiting anyone else.

Their grandfather looked very regal, sitting in his tall-backed armchair wearing his navy blue mandarin robe. He managed local administrative affairs until the Nationalist Government came into power. Phoenix's great grandfather had many children but only one son, so all of his possessions went to Elder Wong when he passed away. Elder Wong inherited 100 *mou* of land as recorded in the ancestral temple, but kept only half and distributed the rest to his sisters' sons, since only males could inherit property.

Elder Wong was very successful in managing his wealth and earned enough rent from his tenant farmers to be the wealthiest man in the village. He had to overcome early setbacks in his personal life when his wife died giving birth to his third son, Phoenix's father, and subsequently the deaths of his first two sons. The birth of his grandson had brought him immense pride and comfort.

He smiled as he watched his granddaughters entertain their baby brother by blowing on their colourful lucky windmills from the temple. Choy was still too young to play with his sisters, but he looked happy nonetheless.

'*Gong hei fat choy!*' A familiar voice broke Elder Wong's concentration. It was his classmate Elder Cheng from the neighbouring village. Both went to the same local school; Elder Cheng passed the provincial examination but it was Elder Wong who went on to be an Imperial graduate and start a bureaucratic career.

Elder Cheng was indebted to Elder Wong, as the Wongs paid

for his school fees when his father ran out of money. Even though he spent most of his time in Guangdong as an education official, Elder Cheng never failed to visit his dear friend Elder Wong when he was back in the village. Since his retirement, Elder Cheng decided to spend his time teaching local children.

'Congratulations on your grandson. He looks like a fine boy. No doubt he will grow up to be a great man like his grand-father!'

'All thanks to your blessings! Cheng, you're looking fine yourself. Always so full of energy like when we were boys. My grandson Choy will have a lot to learn from you.'

'I see the boy has a name now – Choy is a very good name. He will add to the wealth of the Wong family. I wonder when I will have the good fortune to play with my grandson. My son Long is still so young, all because I married so late.'

'All things will come in their own time. No doubt a man of your standing will be surrounded by grandchildren in the prime of your life.'

'I have been lucky in my career. Thanks to the gods I had benefactors like your father who looked out for me. I hope my son will be as fortunate. We live in uncertain times. There has been widespread unrest since Yuan Shikai proclaimed himself the Emperor of China.'

'Let's not talk about matters of state today – how about a game of chess while we wait for my other guests to turn up?' Elder Wong turned the conversation to their favourite pastime.

The kitchen was busy the whole week leading up to New Year's Day, preparing a feast to remember. Wong spared no expense in throwing a lavish banquet of chicken, duck, geese, fish and pig to celebrate the birth of his first son. Even Phoenix and Jade helped out by dyeing red eggs that would be given to the guests to symbolise happiness and fertility.

In past years, the family observed a vegetarian diet for the first three days of New Year to cleanse their body in keeping with the

15

Buddhist tradition. All the food was prepared before New Year since sharp objects like knives were considered unlucky. Wong made an exception this year because it was his son's hundredth day celebration.

By dusk, the banquet was in full swing. Large lanterns lit up the south end of the ancestral temple where the opera stage was located. Waiters were shuttling between the temporary dining area and the kitchen with food and alcohol. Even though the banquet was mainly for the adults, there was a table set up for the children of visiting relatives.

'Why do *we* have to sit with the other children? We should sit with our father at the host table,' Jade whined.

'Well, someone has to host the children. Father will be pleased if we do a good job,' Phoenix comforted Jade.

'All right, it doesn't sound too bad if you put it that way. Anyway, I just noticed that Elder Cheng's son, Long, is also at the children's table, even though he is much older than us. That should make it more interesting!'

Unfortunately, their table was farthest away from the opera stage.

'Big Sister, let's go backstage to see the actors put on their make-up. Maybe we can persuade one of them to let us try on their sparkling costumes and headpieces.'

'Hold on, Jade. You know women aren't allowed on stage.[2]'

'Don't worry, our father is paying for the performance, I'm sure they won't mind.'

Indeed Master Li, the head of the troupe, recognised they were Wong's children and turned a blind eye.

Phoenix and Jade were not the only children on stage. There were boys who were sold by their poor parents to the opera troupe so they could learn a skill and earn their keep. Some of the older ones had small acrobatic roles to perform, while the others ran errands for the actors. The master of props, Master

---

[2] Male actors took on both the male and female roles.

Wu, was keeping a watchful eye on the girls to see they didn't get in the way.

'If you can get me a roast goose leg and some rice wine, I'll give you a prop to play with.'

'No problem, you can count on me!' answered Jade – but it was Phoenix who had to convince the cook to give up a piece of good meat.

For their reward, Master Wu gave them a horsewhip fashioned from a thin piece of rattan, decorated with coloured silk and tassels. Jade was thrilled. Off stage, she swung the whip and pretended she was Mulan on her horse galloping to war. Master Wu noticed Phoenix didn't seem to mind that Jade wanted the new toy all to herself.

'You're a sensible girl not to fight with your sister. Your sister has a mole on her right cheek, which means she's prone to jealousy. You may not always be able to give in to your sister's desires – but do think about the repercussions if you ever cross her.'

It was an odd piece of advice that Phoenix did not understand until later in life.

2

Match Made in Heaven

Phoenix was enjoying her novel in the garden when her sister interrupted her quiet afternoon. Reading was her only respite from the hustle and bustle of living in a multi-generational household.

'Jie, Third Aunt is here again, no doubt with more proposals from Gold Mountain guests[3]. Why don't you settle on one of them? I'm sure they are all very eligible bachelors. Don't you want to experience life in the West?' Jade was selfishly motivated as she had to stay single as long as her elder sister was unmarried.

These 'Gold Mountain' bachelors were single men who made their money in San Francisco during the gold rush and were looking to find a bride back in their hometown.

'It is up to Ba-ba and Ma-ma to decide who my husband will be. I don't have an opinion on this matter. If I had a choice I would like to stay close to home instead of marrying far away,' said Phoenix in an unemotional tone.

'That's going to be hard. So many of our good men have joined the Nationalists. The ones left behind are either too old or too poor to get married,' interjected Third Aunt, who had wandered into the garden unannounced. 'I think your father has someone in mind for you though. He has turned down all my proposals so far.'

---

[3] Early Chinese immigrants to the United States were drawn to the discovery of gold in California and were thus referred to as Gold Mountain guests.

Third Aunt was not a relative of the Wong's but a matchmaker who knew everyone's business. Both girls were stunned by her sudden appearance. They were careful not to give her too much fodder for her to spread gossip around town.

'Third Aunt, it is so nice of you to visit our parents. Please have a seat. Have you had lunch yet?' Phoenix was the first to break the awkward silence. Although she was indignant that an outsider had been listening in on their private conversation, Third Aunt was still a guest and needed to be treated as such.

'Thank you, Phoenix. You have such good manners and know how to treat old people well. Any family would be lucky to have you as a daughter-in-law. Not like your cousin Hailin – she has a sour demeanour and was born in the year of the Tiger. It's not a surprise that your uncle died young. No one wants to marry a difficult wife who will bring bad luck to the family.'

Matchmakers were known to be glib talkers who could distort the truth to their advantage. Third Aunt was usually very diplomatic but was frustrated that she had been unsuccessful in getting Hailin a husband. It was a blemish on her otherwise perfect record.

'Such nonsense! I'm also born in the year of the Tiger. My parents are still alive. I'm sure I will make a good wife.' Third Aunt's careless remarks touched a raw nerve with Jade.

'I don't mean that, my dear girl. You are blessed with your father's wealth and your mother's good looks. We'll have no problems finding you a good man. I will go and talk to your father about your marriage prospects.' Third Aunt made a hasty retreat.

That evening, Jade was still fuming about what Third Aunt said. 'Can you believe the gall of that woman, making such snide remarks about our family? Who does she think she is? I told Baba but he just laughed and said I shouldn't take such things to heart. I'm going for a walk to clear my head otherwise I'll never sleep tonight.'

19

'It's the seventh month. I don't think you should go out alone, especially after dark. I'll come with you.' Phoenix was reluctant to break the house rules but she knew her sister always did whatever she felt like.

'I think my anger would chase away the hungry ghosts. Don't worry – I won't be long. I'm just taking a short walk along the river.'

'I won't be able to sleep till you come home, so don't stay out too late!' Phoenix was still uneasy, but gave in to her sister.

It was almost mid autumn. The moon's large orange reflection danced on the river like the golden yolk in a mooncake.

Guided by the moonlight, Jade quietly left the Wong residence by the back door and crossed a footbridge over the river to the trail that ran beside the village. This pathway was seldom used as it had a tendency to turn into a river of mud when it rained but it was now dry season, so Jade didn't have to worry about getting her silk slippers dirty.

When they were children, Phoenix and Jade used to spend hours on the trail with Fatty, catching butterflies and playing hide-and-seek among the tall rushes along the path. There were no butterflies at this hour, just cicadas singing to attract their mates. The deafening sound stopped momentarily as Jade came close, resuming again when they had flown to the next tree.

Jade looked behind her, just in case she was being followed, before cutting through rushes where a red marker stood. She walked a short distance to a clearing where a tall silhouette stood waiting for her. It was her lover, Long.

Long's father, Elder Cheng, was Jade's grandfather Elder Wong's close friend but they had not had a chance to meet each other from the night of Choy's hundredth day celebration until Elder Wong passed away. At his funeral, Jade noticed a young man smiling at her. She couldn't help smiling back, even though she was in mourning.

Since Long came with Elder Cheng, it wasn't hard to guess

who he was. Jade was taken by his good looks. He had a scholarly air about him like Liang Shangbo in *The Butterfly Lovers*, but with broad shoulders like Wu Song in *Outlaws of the Marsh*. She had heard Choy talk about his schoolteacher Long but never paid much attention, as she remembered him to be a scrawny and pimply-faced boy.

After the funeral he began to drop by the Wong residence to help Choy with his homework and was often invited to have dinner with the family. On one such occasion, Long slipped a note to Jade.

Dear Jade,
I am sorry to be so bold but I can't stop thinking of you. My life is dull and colourless without your presence. I go about my life in a routine every day. The highlight is when I see you at your father's home, yet it is only ever for a few fleeting moments. If you give me a chance, I would like to see you alone so I can be more to you than just your brother's teacher.

That was the beginning of their secret romance.

No one suspected a thing as Jade would go for her walks before he left the Wong residence. As a single woman from a respectable family, she knew she wasn't allowed to go out with a man unchaperoned. She was flattered by Long's attention and convinced herself that if he did find out, her father would approve of their relationship.

Their meetings were always brief to avoid any suspicion. They spent their precious time together sharing childhood memories and talking about their family life and aspirations. Jade was anxious to make their relationship known to her family but Long asked her to be patient. He said he needed more time to prepare his parents for the news.

On this night, after the earlier encounter with Third Aunt, Jade couldn't help but bring up the topic of marriage again.

'Ah-Long, do you love me?' asked Jade after she ran into his arms.

'Of course I do, you are my little wife! I will prove it with my kisses.' Long promptly made good on his promise.

Jade was not in the mood that night for sweet talk. 'I want more than kisses. I want to be your wife in name. I was insulted this afternoon by Third Aunt who said I wouldn't be able to find a husband because I'm born in the year of the Tiger.'

'That Third Aunt is an ignorant woman who talks too much. When the time is right my parents will send our matchmaker to propose marriage. I swear by the moon that I will make you my wife.' Long raised his right hand and held Jade's palm to his chest with his left.

This was the confirmation Jade was looking for. She was moved beyond words.

'We should seal the vow with a kiss.' Long drew her close for a passionate kiss.

This was not the first time they had kissed. In the past, Jade allowed Long to kiss her on the lips but didn't kiss him back. She heard from servants that you could get pregnant from eating a man's saliva. This time she decided to throw caution to the wind and kissed him back.

As their tongues made contact, she was eager to have more. Long cradled her in his arms as they lay on the grass. She could see the moon and the stars as they kissed as if they were the cowherd and the weaver girl meeting across the Milky Way.

In the height of passion, Long's hands wandered down the side of her cheongsam to where the slit revealed her naked thighs. While she wanted to be desired, she didn't know what to expect. She had seen dogs mate and there was nothing romantic about that. She blushed at the thought that Long was going to thrust his male organ into her from behind like a dog.

'No,' she protested and squeezed her legs together to prevent Long's hands from travelling further.

'Don't be scared ... You're my wife, I will take care of you.

Let me show you how couples express their love.' Long persisted and caressed her inner thighs to relax her.

She let out a moan as his fingers gently probed the moist spot between her legs.

Looking into his eyes, Jade said to Long, 'I trust you.'

Phoenix was waiting in Jade's room when she came back and was immediately suspicious when she spotted grass in her hair.

'What have you been doing?'

'I was chasing fireflies. Do you remember how we used to be so carefree and could run around the grassland all afternoon? Now we have to stay home like Chang'e trapped on the moon.'

'We're not children anymore. We should behave like young ladies. I know you're still angry about what Third Aunt said. Don't worry – Ba-ba will find you a good husband but in the meantime, just be thankful he provides for us so we don't need to work like other girls.'

'Well, I'm curious who Ba-ba has in mind for you. He must be the son of one of Ba-ba's business acquaintances. I think it's Uncle Lam's son who we met at the Lantern Festival since we haven't been introduced to anyone else since. Cook told me that the Lam family keeps to old traditions. The boy was betrothed at five but his wife died before they reached marriageable age.'

'Cook can compete with Third Aunt for the number one gossip in the village. I don't remember Uncle Lam's son but I respect Ba-ba's wishes on whom I should marry. As the saying goes, "Marry a chicken, follow a chicken. Marry a dog, follow a dog"!'

'We're no longer living in Imperial China. Why can't we choose whom we marry?'

Phoenix didn't share her sister's notions of free love and made her views clear. 'That's not going to happen in our generation. Instead of wasting time on such foolish thoughts you should honour Ba-ba by behaving like a proper lady. You wouldn't want to attract idle talk from people like Third Aunt.'

Jade fought the urge to tell her sister about Long. She never kept any secrets from Phoenix but she had agreed with Long that it was best to keep their relationship private till the formal marriage proposal, so there would be no doubts about her chastity.

Third Aunt's hunch was right. Phoenix's father did have someone in mind to be her husband. Her mother Ling called her to her bedroom the following night.

'Ma-ma, you've been working hard. Let me give you a shoulder rub.' Without waiting for her mother to respond, she proceeded to give her massage.

'You can read my mind. Third Aunt paid us a visit again yesterday. She was representing the Mas, a friend of your father's from Toishan. Their son has a profitable restaurant business in San Francisco's Chinatown and sent money home to build a two-story house and take a wife.

'They're a good family but your father and I don't want you to be living apart from your husband for an extended period of time. No one knows when Chinese migrants will be allowed to bring their wives to America.'

Phoenix listened attentively without interrupting her mother. She noticed something different on her mother's dresser. It was a jewelry box made from redwood, decorated with ivory inlays.

'You are my dear daughter and we have other plans for you. What do you think of Long?'

Phoenix was caught by surprise. She never thought of Long as anything other than Choy's schoolteacher. Now she understood why Long had been welcomed by her parents as a frequent guest.

'Your grandfather betrothed you to Cheng's son when he was still alive – it's unfortunate that he died before he could see you married. Now that you are of marriageable age we want to fulfill your grandfather's wishes of bringing the two families together.'

'I will honour Ye-ye's wishes,' said Phoenix, as it would be expected of her. She knew this was the next stage in her life journey and felt well prepared by her mother to be a good wife. She had already embroidered a chest full of shoes, socks and bed linens as part of her own dowry.

'That's what I like to hear! Your father and Elder Cheng will decide on the betrothal day. You can share the good news with your sister.'

It was Choy who broke the news to Jade. Choy had grown from a rambunctious baby to a hot-tempered, impetuous teenager who preferred fighting crickets to reading his books. He was treated like a little emperor at home and expected preferential treatment in school. He often got into unprovoked fights. When he lost, he complained to his mother who then went to the schoolmaster demanding that the other child be punished.

Choy lagged behind in his studies, even with Long as a private tutor. Instead of spending time on homework, he hung out in back alleys with village boys betting on crickets, spending his pocket money carelessly. When he ran out of money he turned to his second sister Jade, who would gladly share her allowance without telling on him.

For that reason, he was loyal to Jade and willing to run errands for her, even though he wouldn't lift a finger for anyone else. He didn't share Jade's devotion to Phoenix as he saw her as a half-sister who reminded him of his father – stern and tight-fisted.

Choy wasn't surprised when he found out from his mother that Phoenix was getting married to Long. He was suspicious when Long started giving him special after-school attention. Choy hoped that once Long was successful in getting Phoenix's hand in marriage, he wouldn't be coming around anymore under the pretext of giving tuition.

He went looking for Jade to confirm his theory.

'Second Sister, have you heard from Mother that we're expecting a happy event?'

'She can't be expecting a child at her age!' Jade suspected it was news about Phoenix's wedding, but loved teasing her younger brother.

'Not that kind of happy event ... I'm talking about Big Sister's wedding. I overheard Mother arranging for the betrothal party but she told me not to tell anyone until Father announced the news.'

'Well, I'm not just anyone. I'm family. Why hasn't Phoenix told me herself? She must be afraid I would tease her. So who is the groom? Is he anyone we know?'

'You've met him many times. It is schoolteacher Long. I thought it was strange that he suddenly decided to be my tutor. He was probably looking for opportunities to meet Phoenix. Now that Father has accepted his proposal to Phoenix, do you think he will stop giving me tuition?'

Jade was in a daze. She didn't hear anything her brother said except that the groom was her beloved Long. He said he would marry her – he couldn't have lied. She had given him her virginity.

Did Cheng's matchmaker make a mistake? Maybe she said the proposal was for Miss Wong, first daughter of the family when she meant to say Miss Wong, second daughter of the family. A hundred and one possibilities went through her head. Not once did she question Long's faithfulness.

'Jie, did you hear what I said? Do you think Long will stop giving me tuition?'

'I don't know. This news is a surprise to me. Let me find out the details from your big sister and talk to you later.' Jade struggled to keep her composure and promptly ushered her brother out of her room so she wouldn't alarm him with her sudden tears.

Once behind closed doors she cried long and hard into her pillow, afraid of losing her love. For the past few days she'd been in high spirits, imagining herself as Mrs Cheng. How could things go so wrong? She was desperate to speak to Long but he wasn't due to visit the house for another week.

She had no choice but resort to using Fatty to deliver a letter on the pretext that it was a message from her mother regarding Choy's lessons, so he had no reason to suspect a secret liaison. Jade asked Long to meet her that night, as they needed to talk about something very important.

It was a blessing her father didn't talk about the proposal over dinner that night as Jade was still in a poor state. She feigned illness as an excuse for her lack of appetite. All she could think of was Long – surely he would be able to assure her that the misunderstanding would be resolved and that she was still his bride?

'I would rather you leave the table than see you pick at your food. You're making me lose my appetite,' Wong complained. Even with the happy news, he had a short fuse when it came to bad table manners.

'Jade, why don't you go back to your room to rest? I will come and check on you later,' Mei urged her daughter.

It was exactly what Jade had wanted so that she could slip away from the house, but her cover would be blown if her mother discovered that she wasn't in her bedroom.

'Don't worry, Mother. I'll be fine once I get some sleep.'

Instead of going to bed, she headed to her rendezvous point to meet Long. He was there, waiting for her under their tree. Long was a perfect specimen of a man – tall, good-looking, well bred and educated – someone who would make a good husband and father. She wanted to kiss him and wake up from this nightmare.

'Long, something terrible has happened!'

'What's wrong?' Long rushed forward to embrace Jade.

'Mother told Choy that you are going to marry Phoenix. How can that be?' She wanted Long to tell her that it was just a stupid mistake and he was going to make things right.

Holding Jade tightly to his chest, Long said the unthinkable. 'I'm sorry. I have let you down.'

'What do you mean? You can't possibly have something to do

with this!' Jade was bewildered. She couldn't believe what she was hearing. Long had apologised, as if he had a part in this matter.

'Your grandfather and my father arranged this marriage many years ago. I didn't learn about this till my mother brought it up after your grandfather's funeral. My parents and your parents want to fulfill your grandfather's wishes to bring the two families together. I have been waiting for an opportunity to talk to my father to suggest marrying you instead, I swear I didn't know they went ahead with the proposal without telling me. It may be too late now to change our fate.'

Jade felt hurt that Long had been keeping this secret from her all along, not to mention extremely angry and disappointed that he made such a weak attempt to defend his love.

'You have to tell your parents tonight that you want to marry me and not Phoenix – I've given you my heart and body. You said that I'm your wife but you've been using me all along!'

'Jade, don't get so emotional. I have true feelings for you and still want you to be my wife. I'll talk to my parents and get them to change their minds. Let's make up with a kiss, everything will be all right.'

Jade was sullen and squirmed in Long's arms as he tried to kiss her. His breathing became more intense. The more she resisted the more he wanted her. Her anger turned into panic. Who was this man who professed to love her but was taking advantage of her in her most vulnerable state?

'No, please don't do this ... I have to go home now otherwise my parents will notice that I'm missing,' Jade pleaded.

'You said you want to be my wife. A wife has to please her husband anytime he wants. Show me how much you love me.' He forcefully guided her hands downwards to where she could feel his stiff manhood. 'You need to make me feel good.'

Jade was in shock. This was not what she expected of Long, but she wanted to please him. She was afraid that if she refused, he would think she didn't love him enough and so not want her as his bride.

Swallowing her sobs, Jade complied.

A week passed, but still no news from Long. Jade sent Long another note to meet at their usual place, but he failed to turn up.

She felt frantic and helpless. She tried to act as normal as possible so no one would suspect anything was wrong, pretending to be excited when her father announced her sister's betrothal and even accompanying her mother and sister to the city to get their outfits tailored for the wedding ceremony.

Although her feelings for Long were marred by their last encounter, she couldn't think of marrying anyone else since she had given him her virginity. To make matters worse, she had missed her monthly period and suspected that she was pregnant.

She couldn't confirm it without seeing a doctor but dared not take the risk of anyone finding out. She would be branded a 'loose woman' and her father would probably disown her. She had too much to lose; Long had to marry her.

Jade had no idea if Long had talked to his parents and if so, what the outcome was. She was going to take matters into her own hands and plead her case with Phoenix. After all, her sister was her closest friend.

'My good sister, will you promise to help me?' Jade sought out her sister in the privacy of her room, far from the prying ears of the many relatives who lived in the big house.

'You are my only sister. I'm always here to help you.'

'You have to tell Father that you can't marry Long.'

Phoenix stared at Jade in disbelief.

'I can't do that! The marriage is already arranged with the Chengs – I can't disobey our parents. Why don't you want me to marry Long?'

'Long and I are in a relationship. He promised to marry me

but his parents went ahead with the marriage proposal without his knowledge.'

'Jade, how could this happen? Have you been meeting Long privately during your evening walks? Father will be furious if he finds out. Why did you not tell me sooner?' Phoenix was appalled.

'I was afraid you would disapprove. It wouldn't matter once we were married – I didn't expect this to spin out of control! I don't know who else I can turn to. You have to help me!'

'Is there anything else you're not telling me? What's the extent of your relationship with Long?'

'Please don't pressure me. I'm too ashamed to talk about it.'

'Did he take advantage of you? Look at me Jade – I need to know. I'm supposed to marry this man.'

After a long silence, Phoenix finally spoke without looking up. 'I gave myself willingly ...' She couldn't bear to tell her sister that she may also be pregnant.

'If he is a gentleman he should respect your chastity. He has done a terrible thing. I will tell Father that he needs to act in an honourable way – to marry you.'

'No! Please Big Sister! No ... Father will disown me if he finds out what happened.'

'It will be impossible to explain why I want Long to marry you instead of me, but I'll try my best to persuade them.'

'You're my only hope, I'm counting on you. Otherwise my life will be in ruins!'

Phoenix sighed.

The betrothal gifts were due to be delivered in less than a week, which meant they were a month away from the wedding ceremony. If she called off the engagement, there was no guarantee that Long would marry her sister and her father could lose face. It was a delicate situation.

That night Phoenix told her parents that after careful consideration, she didn't want to marry Long and felt that Jade would make a better daughter-in-law for the Chengs. As expected, her parents couldn't comprehend why she'd had a change of mind.

'I don't understand what's come over you. Tell me the truth. Is there someone else you have in mind? We have already agreed to the proposal! As for Jade, we will find her a good husband but right now the Chengs want you as the bride, not her!' Ling tried to talk sense into her daughter.

'No, Mother. There isn't anyone else. I don't think I'm ready for marriage. I don't want you or Father to lose face. Jade will make a good bride. Everyone knows she is the most beautiful girl in the village and …'

Before she could finish her sentence, her father interrupted her. 'Phoenix, you're not making any sense. Your grandfather proposed this marriage and you are being disrespectful by not fulfilling his wishes. I have been lenient with you as children but don't think that you can now do whatever you wish.'

Realising his words were harsh, he added, 'We care for you and want you to have the best. You may have other ideas about what you want, but we have eaten more salt than you have rice. We are here to guide you with our experience so you will have an easier path.'

Phoenix realised she was fighting a lost cause. She risked losing her parents' trust and affection by going against their will. She had no choice but to tell them the truth.

'Father, Jade is in love with Long and they want to be married to each other. I don't want to stand in the way. Please give them your blessing.'

Both Wong and Ling were visibly shocked by her revelation. After a moment of silence, Wong lashed out at his wife. 'It's your fault that the girls lack any sense of what is right. How dare your daughters talk about romantic love? Tell your sister and your second mother to see us immediately!'

*   *   *

Jade, who was waiting anxiously in Phoenix's room, did not get the good news she hoped for.

'Jade, I'm sorry – it didn't do any good. I told them about you and Long in the hope that they would change their minds. Father wants to talk to you and your mother now.'

Jade was so distraught she didn't know what to do but cry.

'Please don't cry! It breaks my heart to see you so upset.'

'I trusted you with my secret. You're my sister! How can you go back on your word? Father will kill me. If he doesn't, I have no means to support myself if he throws me out.'

'Please understand that I had no choice. I don't want to take the man you love from you, but I thought by telling Father I may be able to stop the wedding. Maybe your mother can help intervene.'

Jade's mother Mei came in. 'I've been looking all over for you! Your father is very angry. What have you done?'

'Mother, you have to help me. Long and I are in love. He cannot marry Big Sister. Please help me plead my case to Father!'

'Oh Jade, how can you get yourself into such trouble? You should have told me sooner. I would have told you to end the relationship. Your grandfather arranged this marriage with the Chengs many years ago. He has always intended Phoenix to be their daughter-in-law. You have to ask for your father's forgiveness and respect his decision. As your father, his will is final.'

Jade tearfully accepted her mother's advice.

Accompanied by her mother and sister, Jade faced the wrath of her father.

His face was as black as his patron god, Guan Gong. Even Phoenix's mother Ling knew better than to further aggravate her husband by speaking up for her half-daughter. She sat quietly in a corner and thumbed her prayer beads in search of divine intervention.

Jade was terrified – and with good reason. As soon as she stepped in the room, Wong slapped her without warning.

'You have shamed our ancestors by your lack of propriety!'

As tears ran down her stinging cheek, Jade kneeled before her father. 'I am sorry to let you down. I admit my mistakes. Please forgive me. Long and I have true feelings for each other. Please don't separate us.'

'How dare you talk about feelings! What about my feelings as a father? I have fed you, clothed you, given you a roof over your head and this is how you repay me – with disobedience! Long is going to be your brother-in-law. You should end any communication with him. We cannot risk your sister's future because of your improper behaviour. The wedding will go ahead as planned. If you know what's good for you, you will not create any more trouble. Otherwise I will disown you!'

Jade knew her father meant what he said and was resigned to her fate.

'Now get out of the room. I don't want to see your face again tonight.'

Jade was emotionally drained. There had been no support from her sister or mother and she felt very alone. She hoped that Long could get his parents to change their minds so they could be reunited.

In the days that followed, Phoenix found a growing distance between herself and her sister. Jade withdrew into her shell and refused to talk. Phoenix was an unwilling bride but expected her sister to understand that she was only obeying her parents' wishes.

She wrote letters to Jade and slipped them under her door.

Dear Jade,
You are the nearest and dearest to my heart. We have shared the best days of our lives growing up together and I am here to share your darkest hour. I would do anything within my powers to see you smile and laugh again.

If I can speak my mind freely, Long is not a good man if he took advantage of your innocence. He may be my future husband but I do not respect what he has done.

Please don't give up on yourself. Father's anger will cool over time and no doubt he will find you a good husband.

I am here for you when you are ready to talk.

Your sister,

Phoenix.

Jade sent a letter in reply.

I have one request. If you are my sister, you will do this for me. On the wedding day, you will switch places with me and let me wear your bridal gown. No one will know the true identity of the bride until the bridegroom lifts my red veil after the ceremony. I will be forever indebted to you if you can grant my wish.

Upon receiving the letter, Phoenix went to Jade's room and knocked on the closed door.

'Jade, let me in. We have to talk.'

She heard a shuffling noise in the room and called to her sister again. 'Jade, please let me in.'

Without opening the doors, Jade asked, 'So have you decided to help me?'

'I want to help you but you are asking for something impossible. I cannot deceive our parents.'

'What solution do you have then? None, I suppose. You don't really want to help me. You would rather be the good daughter and see me suffer. What kind of sister are you? All of you claim to care about me but you really just care about yourselves.'

'Please be rational, Jade. I care about you and so do our parents. Mother said that they did talk to the Chengs, but they refused to hear a word about you and Long. If they cancel the marriage altogether, it would be a great loss of face for our family – so the wedding must go ahead as planned.'

Phoenix tactfully left out the fact that the Chengs wanted their future daughter-in-law to be the daughter of the main wife, not the secondary wife. The Chengs felt Long was not really serious about Jade, he would get over his infatuation. Phoenix, being more mature and stable, would be a better partner for him in the long run.

'You can go ahead with your wonderful lives – you and Long. You are a match made in heaven. You have both hurt me deeply and I will never forgive you.'

3

Marriage and Growing Up

The hair combing ceremony was the night before the wedding day. It was obvious to her mother that Phoenix was preoccupied.

'You look unhappy, my dear daughter,' Ling said to Phoenix as they shared a quiet moment in the bedroom.

'I miss Jade dearly. Under different circumstances, she would be the one being blessed by you and Father. I wonder how she is doing in Canton.'

'Jade will be fine with your aunt. It is better that she stays away. Otherwise it would be awkward for your future in-laws, and for us. I've told everyone that she is recuperating from a serious illness,' Ling comforted Phoenix. 'Now cheer up, your father will be here soon. You wouldn't want to remind him of the unhappy incident, would you?'

'No, I wouldn't!' Phoenix managed a smile just as Wong walked in.

'Are you two leaving me out of your little secret?' Wong teased his daughter and wife.

'My dear husband, you are all-knowing. There is nothing to hide from you. Let's not banter and miss the auspicious hour.'

Wong blessed Phoenix while Ling combed her hair four times.

'May your marriage last a lifetime. May you be blessed with happiness and harmony. May you be blessed with many children and grandchildren. May you live to a ripe old age.'

After the fourth blessing, Wong said to his daughter,

'Tomorrow is your big day. Much as I am sad to see you leave me, I'm happy that you're marrying into a good family. You have always been my favourite child. Your brother and sister have given me nothing but worry and grief – but you are all blessings from the gods. Your mother and I have prepared a generous dowry so your in-laws know how much we cherish you.'

Wong gave Phoenix the lacquer box she had seen in her mother's room the night she first found out about the proposal. In it were four pieces of gold jewelry – a bracelet, a pair of earrings, a necklace and a ring[4]. The heavy gold bracelet was carved in the design of a dragon and phoenix chasing each other in the clouds, to signify love and harmony.

'Once you cross over the threshold of the Cheng household, your body and spirit belong to the Chengs. Don't bring up the past. Obey your husband and be filial to your parents-in-law.'

Even then, Phoenix struggled to come to terms with her misgivings about Long. The man she was going to marry not only took advantage of her sister but also lacked the backbone to stand up for his actions. She wondered what debts the two sisters owed Long in their past lives that they had to repay him in this one at the cost of their sisterly love.

She knew that she had to respect and trust Long if they were going to spend a lifetime together. She looked to her mother as a role model. Like most women, her mother met her father for the first time on their wedding night. Despite being strangers when they were first married, they had a harmonious relationship.

Ling could tell that Phoenix had a lot on her mind.

'My dear daughter, don't think too much! Be a happy bride and bring good fortune to your husband.'

On her parents' advice, Phoenix decided to bury the past and move forward with her new life.

---

4   Dowry was typically given to daughters as a compensation for not inheriting any of their father's estate.

*   *   *

Phoenix was filled with trepidation on her wedding night.

After the wedding banquet, she waited for her husband in the bridal chambers, still dressed in her wedding cheongsam. She absentmindedly played with the dragon phoenix bracelet on her wrist as she thought of her father and mother and sister. Through her veil, she looked around the room that was going to be her new home. It was decorated with calligraphy and paintings that hinted at the family's scholarly lineage.

It seemed like hours before her husband stumbled in with his friends, reeking of alcohol. The rowdy young men wanted to tease the couple with raucous games before they consummated their marriage. It was something Phoenix hadn't expected. Thankfully, her father-in-law intervened as Long was clearly too drunk to participate in the typical wedding night banter.

As soon as the crowd left, Phoenix closed the door and tended to her husband who was already snoring on the bed, still dressed in his wedding jacket and trousers. She took care of him as she would her brother. She was careful not to wake him as she washed his face, took off his shoes and lifted his legs onto the bed.

She had a sense of temporary relief that she didn't need to do 'the man/woman thing' with Long that night. She blew out the candle, took off her wedding gown in the dark and crept into bed next to Long.

Unfortunately, Long did not sleep through the night. When he woke up and pulled Phoenix so close to him she could smell his sour breath, Phoenix couldn't help but feel disgusted that he had taken her sister's virginity and now he would take hers.

She knew it was her duty as a wife to serve her husband's needs. She mentally prepared herself to give herself up to him in order to produce a son. After they fumbled silently to get undressed in the dark, Long touched every part of her naked body and then climbed on top of her.

Phoenix waited for the inevitable, but it didn't happen. Long was too drunk.

There is a Chinese proverb that says 'No waves without wind'. Rumours surfaced after Jade was visibly absent from the celebrations.

'Mei, I have to ask you a delicate question,' said Ling. 'Do you know if anything happened between Jade and Long?'

'Big Sister, I was as much in the dark about their relationship as you were. Why are you bringing this up now?'

'I overheard Fatty telling the cook that someone saw Jade with a man by the river. They suspect that Jade was sent away to hide an unwanted pregnancy. I was furious and told them to stop such gossip.'

'Mei, how can you let this happen? Jade is such a disgrace …' Suddenly, Wong surprised them by walking in on their conversation. He was furious.

'I knew you women were hiding something from me!'

'Please don't get worked up. It is just a rumour,' said Ling, trying to pacify her husband.

'How can I not be angry? This kind of vicious talk will tarnish our family's reputation. We need to stop any more speculations. Our only hope now is to marry her off to a good family so that our honour can be restored!' Wong shook his head and walked off in a huff.

Many of the prospective husbands were deterred by the rumours they heard. Although Jade was attractive, no one wanted to marry a non-virgin – 'a broken shoe'. Jade's mother Mei was at her wit's end, when Third Aunt came to her with a suggestion.

'I know you've been worrying about your daughter's future. Remember my proposal from the Mas? They are still looking for a daughter-in-law for their son in San Francisco. They live in Toishan so they wouldn't have heard the rumours … Their son would be a good match for Jade; their birth charts are compatible. As Ma's daughter-in-law, she would gain respect-ability.'

'Thank you, Third Aunt, for thinking of us. This sounds like a good proposition but we all know what the life of a Gold Mountain wife is like. Jade may live like a widow for years before she sees her husband. There's no guarantee that he will not take another wife in America. Without a son to secure her status, she would be powerless.'

'I hope you'll give it serious consideration. If I may be honest, Jade's reputation is now tarnished regardless of whether she is innocent or not. She can't afford to be picky about who she marries. It's much better for her to marry a Gold Mountain guest as a first wife than to become a concubine to an old man.'

That last statement hit a raw nerve with Mei, as she was a concubine. She was fortunate that Ling was kind and generous as a first wife, but often concubines were treated no better than servants.

'I understand that well.'

Jade was thankful that she was sent off to stay with her mother's sister in Canton. She didn't want to have any part in the wedding celebrations. Long and Phoenix were the two people she held closest to her heart, which made their betrayal all the more difficult to bear.

'I am sure you would rather be at the wedding than here with me. I would have gone myself if not for my severe arthritis. Your uncle and your cousins were happy to go without me – I won't be surprised if they get up to some mischief. Have I told you about the time when they ...' Jade's aunt rambled on about some story that was of no interest to her niece.

'Yes, Aunt,' Jade answered, absent-mindedly.

'You know, Jade, your mother is worried about your health. Shutting yourself up in your room all day is not going to do you any good. You should come sit with me in the garden and enjoy the fresh air. I don't mind if you want to go out for a walk. You can take one of the servants with you, if you like.'

Jade was glad that her aunt gave her free rein to do whatever she pleased. She did not probe Jade for the real reason she was in Canton, neither did Jade volunteer any information. She preferred to keep to herself – and for good reason.

She had missed two cycles of her monthly flow and noticed symptoms of pregnancy similar to her mother's when she was expecting Choy. Her breasts were larger and there was even a slight swell in her belly. There was no denying that she was with child.

There was no way Jade could have this baby. Her father had already threatened to disown her because of her relationship with Long. If he knew she had lost her chastity, he would throw her out. She would rather kill herself than beg on the streets.

She convinced herself that she didn't care for the child inside her. With each passing day, it was a growing reminder of how she had been betrayed: she refused to let Long and Phoenix ruin her life more than they already had. The pregnancy had to be ended before anyone found out.

Jade had a plan. She went to a traditional Chinese medicine hall to confirm her worst fears. Since she was a stranger in the city, she lied to the physician that she was newly married. He took her pulse and congratulated her on the pregnancy.

She pretended to be excited about the news and asked if there were any activities she should avoid. She was told not to eat *dong quai*, take hot baths, jump or handle sharp objects ... It was a long list. She visited another medical hall for a prescription to increase blood flow that included *dong quai*, known as women's ginseng. Jade's aunt's servant didn't ask any questions when she was asked to prepare some herbal soup with this prescription. To ensure success, Jade jumped up and down every night until she broke into a sweat and then soaked in hot baths.

After a week, she experienced intense cramps as she was

taking a bath. It was unlike any pain she had ever felt. It was as though her unborn child was punishing her for being a bad mother. As her body contorted with spasms, she broke into a cold sweat, despite the heat of the water.

She felt like passing out from the pain, but she had to stay conscious. She could not let anyone know what was happening.

'Please help me Guan Yin, Goddess of Mercy. This pain is unbearable ... Please don't punish me for what I am doing, I have no choice. This child will have no future. I don't want to be a murderer!' Jade sobbed.

When she stood up with much effort, she felt a warm rush of fluid run down her legs. Long's child was bleeding through her.

Soon, there was nothing left inside her but bitter tears.

Jade was relieved when she received a letter from her mother. Her first thought was that her father missed her after all and wanted her home.

Dear Daughter,
I trust you are well. We have found you a good match, I am happy for you. The groom is from a reputable family in Toishan. Your father would like you to return home immediately.

Jade's heart sank like a rock as she read the letter. It seemed she had no choice in the matter. Her fate was already sealed.

It was only when she went home that she heard about the rumours and realised that she had few options. Respectable families avoid potential daughter-in-laws with a chequered past. She could stay single but she would be living on the goodwill of her parents and her brother, once he inherited her father's wealth.

Her mother prepared her for the challenges she would face with an absentee husband.

'My dear daughter, I know this marriage is not one you hoped for but you have to make the most of it.' Ling became tearful at the thought of Jade's lonely future.

'Mother, why can't I stay here with you until my husband returns from abroad?' Jade pleaded.

'Once you are married, you will no longer be part of our household. You will be your husband's wife, a daughter-in-law in the Ma family. While your husband is away, you have to live up to your in-laws' expectations as a good wife would. When he returns, make sure you please him as it is your duty to produce a son.'

Jade silently nodded.

Her future husband ran a successful restaurant business in San Francisco. By marrying him, she would gain respectability as a businessman's wife and financial independence from her parents. She didn't have romantic notions of falling in love with a man she hadn't met. There was no room in her heart for love, just hatred for the two people who had caused her misery.

She was pleased that her husband spared no expense on the wedding, from the betrothal gifts to the lavish banquet. Even her father was visibly proud of his new son-in-law. It made up in some extent for the loss of face. It would have been a perfect wedding – except her husband couldn't make it back to China, so Jade was married to the rooster that took his place.

In her bridal chamber, decked out in red paper cuttings of double-happiness, and dragon and phoenix candles, she spent her first of many nights alone.

Jade's married life had an ominous start. Her father-in-law fell ill and passed away not long after her wedding, leaving behind his elderly wife. Even though her husband Tong grieved for his father, he decided not to travel back for the funeral since it would take seventy days to travel from San Francisco by boat. Jade received a letter from him, expressing his expectations of what her role should be.

My Dear Wife,
I am sure the funeral will be over by the time this letter reaches you. It would not have made sense for me to travel back since we could not possibly hold off the burial for such a long time, but I trust you have helped my mother with the arrangements. Please take good care of her. While I am away, you have to run the household in my stead.

The Mas owned land that was rented to tenant farmers. It was now up to Jade to negotiate terms and manage rental earnings.

In Toishan, where no one knew her past, she was seen as the Ma's filial and beautiful daughter-in-law. Jade's head swelled with pride. She lived in the biggest house in the village and dressed well to reflect her social status.

Jade didn't have a good head for numbers, even though her father was a businessman. Since her mother-in-law didn't have any advice on how to manage the finances, Jade spent freely as she knew there would be a steady income from rent, supplemented by remittances from her husband in America.

When her father-in-law was still alive, he travelled to the farms he owned on rent day. His argument was that it made it harder for tenants to be late with their rents if he collected in person. After he died, Jade decided it was beneath her to collect rent and appointed the family caretaker, who was also a distant relative of the Mas, to take up this tedious job.

With the rent collection out of the way, Jade had a lot of free time. There were servants to take care of all housekeeping duties. Jade didn't have to do any real work, just keep her mother-in-law company. She learned to play mahjong so she could jump in when her mother-in-law's mahjong regulars needed a fourth player.

On these outings, Jade met other young daughter-in-laws like herself who were married to overseas husbands. She soon built up a circle of friends who met for social activities, mahjong games and opera.

'Life as a wife of a Gold Mountain guest is not so bad after all!' Jade thought to herself.

With both sisters married and moved out, there was no one to keep an eye on Choy. No matter how many tutors he got over the years, Choy's grades didn't improve. His father was frustrated by the boy's lack of aptitude.

'All our ancestors were scholars. You are a disgrace to our family name. If you can't study, you will need to pick up some skills. I am sending you to your uncle's trading firm as an apprentice in Canton – your uncle and aunt didn't mind hosting Jade all those years ago. Make sure you behave yourself so they don't complain about you.'

'But Father, I don't know anyone in Canton! Why can't I stay here and learn from you instead?'

'You'll be better off with your uncle – I have no patience with you. It'll do you good to experience the real world and build up business contacts in a big city. Do well and make us proud.'

Choy had mixed feelings about leaving his home. Even though he was already fifteen, he enjoyed being pampered by his mothers. On one hand he was excited to explore the big city, but on the other he didn't like change. Living with his uncle meant he needed to be more independent and couldn't have servants to wait on him hand and foot.

The one big relief was that he would not have to study – or pretend to study – anymore.

Like Jade, Choy found that life outside the Wong household exceeded his expectations. His older cousins took him under their wings and showed him city life. He didn't get paid for his apprenticeship with his uncle, but his mothers both sent him pocket money whenever he asked for it.

'We've planned a surprise for your birthday!' announced his cousin Ting. His cousin Wing stood by him with a cheeky grin.

The two boys were nineteen and twenty years old respectively and worked alongside Choy in their father's trading firm. Having been the only boy in his household, he enjoyed the company of his male cousins even though they sometimes bossed him around.

'I'm game for anything!' said Choy. 'Show me what you've got.'

The boys headed off to a part of town that Choy knew to be the red-light district. His father would not approve of such activities but he threw caution to the wind. No one would know, if his cousins didn't tell.

His cousins seemed to know the area very well. As they made their way down a narrow alley, they chatted with heavily made-up women who stood at the doorways of dimly lit houses in body-hugging cheongsams.

Choy found himself gawking at their provocative figures and the side splits that revealed their lily-white thighs. There was even a white woman who was dressed in a similar daring fashion, except her cheongsam was opened at the collar revealing the fullness of her breasts.

'Do you like what you see? We've brought you here to drink flower wine for your birthday,' said Wing, who had his arms around an older woman.

'Big Sister will introduce you to the girls who will keep us company as we drink.'

Once they stepped inside the brothel, the madam arranged for a private room and ordered food and wine. As Wing promised, she ushered in a bevy of girls to keep them company with drinking games.

One of the girls looked like she could have been his age. Big Sister caught him looking at the girl and made the introduction. Her name was Xi Shi. Choy thought she was well named because she was pretty like Xi Shi, one of the four beauties of ancient China.

After several rounds of wine, Ting pushed Choy to the girl and said, 'Take good care of him. He's a spring chicken!'

Choy blushed, as he was indeed a virgin. He didn't know what to expect as Xi Shi led him up the stairs to a sparingly decorated room with a bed, a chamber pot, and a small table with a jug of water and a bowl to wash in. Xi Shi undressed him and took off his shoes with a charming smile.

'Lie back on the bed while I prepare your smoke. It will help you relax and waken your senses, so you can enjoy the experience.'

Through a haze of bluish opium smoke, Choy saw Xi Shi take off her clothes and reveal her naked body. And thus, Choy was initiated into the world of opium smoking and prostitution.

Choy was the happiest he had ever felt in his life. He had a short attention span and didn't do well at work but his uncle still kept him on to do general administration. He looked forward to the end of the day when he would go out with his cousins to the brothels and opium dens.

After his first time, Choy was expected to pay for his own girls and opium. His cousins helped him out to start with, but then refused to go out with him if he couldn't pay. So Choy sent letters home asking for money.

Not realising what mischief Choy was getting up to, his mothers indulged his repeated requests. As Choy got more addicted to opium, he found the money was running out faster than it was coming in. He even pawned a pocket watch that was a gift from his father to support his habits.

Although his cousins warned him not to get addicted to opium, it became hard for Choy to function without smoking. When he was smoking he could forget about his father's high expectations of him. When he was smoking, he was at peace.

He didn't care if he had the company of a prostitute when he had a smoke. Instead of going to brothels, Choy started to visit seedy opium dens where he paid for lower-grade pellets so he could make his money stretch. When his money ran out, he borrowed from opium den owners who took advantage of him.

47

'Of course I can pay for your smoke and I can guarantee we give you the best quality, as long as you can pay back with interest.'

'My father has plenty of money. Of course I can pay you back – it's just that the money hasn't arrived!'

Choy repeated this promise to several opium den owners, without realising the seriousness of the situation. These people were all part of Triad societies, ready to take extreme measures to get their loans and interest back.

When Choy didn't make good on his promise, he was ambushed by thugs outside his uncle's office.

'Hey, Mister! My big brother says you owe him money. Where is it?' Three very fierce-looking men pushed him against a wall as soon as he stepped out of the front door.

'You must have the wrong person. I … don't owe anyone money,' Choy stammered.

'Don't think we are fools. Do you know who we are? You better hand over the money now otherwise I will beat you till you're coughing up blood,' threatened the most intimidating one in the gang, as he tightened his grip around Choy's neck.

'I'm sorry. I don't know what you're talking about!' Choy continued the charade.

The gangsters were so infuriated by his denials that they carried out their threat. Choy was beaten up so badly that blood was pouring out of his mouth from a broken jaw. He was told to expect more severe punishment if he failed to pay within five days.

Instead of being sympathetic, his uncle was unhappy that Choy had mixed with the wrong crowd and drawn unwanted attention to his workplace. He was told to pack up and go home. Even his cousins didn't dare to speak up for him.

At the same time, the moneylenders sent an ultimatum to Wong to settle the outstanding debt on his son's behalf. Otherwise it would be paid in blood. Wong feared for his son's life, but was furious that he was so reckless with his money.

'You must help our son. If you don't help him, no one else will!' begged Mei when Wong broke the news to her. 'Even if he has done something wrong, he's our only son.'

'Dear husband, please take pity on the boy, he's still so young. Yes, we've spoilt him but he doesn't deserve to be punished. I beg you – please pay off the debts! We would regret it for the rest of our lives if he was hurt,' pleaded Ling in earnest, even though Choy was not her flesh and blood.

For Wong, it was a foregone conclusion. 'I will bring him home and discipline him in front of our ancestors.'

The year of 1932 was not a good one for Wong. He had incurred substantial financial losses due to the Great Depression. He now had the added stress of having to pay off his son's opium debts.

Although the Great Depression started in the West, the impact was felt all around the world. Wong's trading business was devastated as business partners defaulted and prices for foreign goods and assets dropped sharply in value. He had inherited a silkworm farm from his father, but demand for raw silk fell so dramatically that he had to sell the farm to the bank to stem his losses.

'How are we going to pull through this crisis?' Wong shook his head and sighed as he reviewed the family expenses.

'At least we still have the roof over our heads and land to bring in some income,' said Ling, trying to comfort him.

'Yes, but the income is not enough for all of us to live on. We have too many mouths to feed.'

'That's true, but we can survive with less. We can cut down on the household expenses by letting some of the servants go,' Ling suggested.

'We can't do that! What would people think?'

'We need to be practical. How about asking our late uncle's wives and children to pay for their room and board?'

'No! That's out of the question. I promised my father I would take care of them. I won't let him down, I'm a man of my word. Let's not bring this up again.'

The stress caused Wong to fall ill. He suffered frequent and severe chest pains. His physician diagnosed that he suffered an imbalance in chi (energy) that caused his chest to tighten whenever he felt anxious.

The physician, an old friend, gave Wong an honest assessment. 'I can improve your chi with acupuncture treatment and herbal medicine but you need to help yourself too. I know you have a lot on your mind but if you don't relax, your heart will not be able to cope.'

'That's easier said than done, but I will try.'

Wong had no choice but to trust Choy with his business.

Wong was not the only one affected by the Depression. As a schoolteacher, Long saw school admissions drop. Families could hardly feed their children, let alone pay tuition. Instead of cash, he was paid 100 *jin* (64 kilograms) of unhusked rice per month which Phoenix traded for other essentials like salt and oil.

Long inherited his father's estate when both his parents succumbed to the pneumonic plague that swept through their village in the winter of 1934. A year later, Phoenix gave birth to a daughter, Jing Jing.

'Our daughter has her mother's good looks,' said Long as he gazed at his firstborn with adoration. 'If only my parents could be here to see her grow up.'

'They are watching over her in their afterlife,' Phoenix comforted her husband.

Long felt that his family was complete when Phoenix gave him a son the following year. Although he never mentioned it to Phoenix, he was remorseful about taking advantage of Jade. He felt fortunate that Phoenix had married him, despite his mistake.

Times were tough and he definitely needed a good wife to stand by his side.

4

Gold Mountain Wife

Jade felt she was a good wife. For the first two years of her so-called marriage, she exchanged regular letters with her husband, whom she had yet to meet. Every so often someone from the *jinshanzhuang*[5] came to her house and informed her that she had mail. She would visit the town to pick up the letters and remittance money and to send letters back to her husband, Tong.

During the Depression, the correspondence became sporadic. With money running low, Jade struggled to maintain the household. She wished she hadn't spent the several hundred gold pieces throwing a lavish seventieth birthday celebration for her mother-in-law.

Honourable Husband,
Winter is fast approaching. I hope you are well and keeping warm.

Mother is in good health but her memory is failing. Every night she insists on putting out an extra portion of food because she thinks you will be home for dinner. She gets very agitated when I tell her that you are still in America.

The physician says that she needs to nourish her kidneys

---

[5] *Jinshanzhuang* or Gold Mountain firms delivered remittance and letters for overseas Chinese.

to curb the side effects of old age. Please send money to pay for the herbs as our funds have run low.

Our tenant farmers have been late on their rent payments because of poor harvests. I entrusted Second Uncle with the rent collection, but he has since disappeared with the money.

Mother and I are dependent on you to survive in these hard times. I hope you will not find me bothersome with my repeated requests for money.

Take care of yourself.

Your wife,

Jade.

For a while, she fooled herself into thinking this situation was only temporary. She heard people say that the economy was bad but she didn't expect to be affected. She swallowed her pride and asked the accountant at the *jinshanzhuang* for a cash advance. Although she hadn't heard from Tong, she felt sure that he would be able to pay up.

'Madam Ma, I would really like to help you but the reality is that we have had many similar requests from other wives and now we have too many bad debts.'

'I'm not like other wives! My husband owns a successful restaurant in San Francisco; he is not some cheap labourer! We have the biggest house in the village. My husband is just too busy to send money.'

'I am a businessman, not a charity organisation. I'm afraid you need to find your money elsewhere.'

Jade was so shocked with his brutally honest response that she stormed out of his office, blushing with humiliation.

It normally took a fortnight for her letter to reach Tong, then another for his reply to reach her. When she didn't receive any reply to her last letter, she thought either Tong had found a new wife in America or something terrible had happened to him. She was left to her own resources to support Madam Ma and herself.

She had grown accustomed to her life of leisure as a Gold Mountain wife. Suddenly, she had to watch her expenses and worry about how to pay the bills. She couldn't get credit from the market for groceries and her servants refused to work unless they were paid.

Her mother-in-law's memory deteriorated and her character transformed from a mild-mannered lady into a loud and abrasive old woman. She frequently blamed Jade for being unfilial.

'It's all because of you that my husband died ... We should have known better than to marry our son to a Tiger wife! My son should divorce you for not honouring our family with a son.'

Mother, please don't shout – the servants are listening. I will honour our family with a son when my husband comes back!'

Jade blamed her mother-in-law for her affair. These daily battles drove her out of the house from sheer exasperation.

Jade had not been with any man since Long. It was flattering to get attention from Sui even if he was an older man, married with children – and grandchildren. He was the husband of one of her mother-in-law's mahjong friends. Sui had made his money in the Philippines and had married a local woman as a second wife.

He had a flamboyant air about him, but his wife didn't seem to mind. She knew about his other family and tolerated his indiscretions, as long as he provided for her and her children.

Jade was very embarrassed when she bumped into Sui as she stepped out of the pawn shop one day. She was there to trade in a pair of jade earrings to pay bills; she had been pawning off small items hoping Madam Ma wouldn't notice. The last thing she wanted was for a family friend to know that they were in need of money.

'What a surprise, Sui! I didn't know you come here to shop, too. There are a lot of bargains … Frankly, I don't see anything wrong with buying second-hand jewelry, if it's of good quality.'

'Don't worry, Jade. I'm not going to tell anyone I saw you here. Your secret's safe with me. This is not a good part of town – let me walk you home.'

Jade didn't think anything untoward about his offer. After all, he was well respected in the village for his generous donations to the local schools. She trusted him as a family friend.

When she arrived home with Sui, Madam Ma didn't recognise him as her friend's husband and thought her son had returned instead. She had the servants prepare all his favourite dishes, despite Jade's protests.

Jade said to Sui apologetically, 'Sorry, my mother-in-law's not well. She misses her son. My husband has not been back for many years!'

'I understand. Old people like me can become forgetful and difficult at times. I'll come by to visit her more often. I'm sure you could do with some male companionship in the house.'

Jade wasn't sure what to make of Sui's last comment.

Since that visit, Sui dropped by frequently and he always brought gifts of food and herbal medicine for her mother-in-law.

'Thank you, Sui. I really appreciate your help in these difficult times.' Jade was very touched by his kind gestures. She was aware that he was interested in her – and didn't resist his advances.

'You are as pretty as a fairy descended from the heavens. You deserve to be adored. I bought you a hairpin that I'm sure you'll like, why don't we go to your room so you can put it on and look at yourself in the mirror?' Jade smiled and led him to her room.

'How do I look?' she asked coyly after placing the pin in her hair.

'You look exquisite, and I'm sure you have a beautiful body to match the beautiful face. Let me see what is under those clothes.'

Jade blushed like a girl and did not stop Sui as he proceeded to undress her. Sui adorned every part of her with tender kisses as an experienced lover would; soon, she was in heaven.

Sui gave her temporary respite from the monetary problems that were plaguing her. In return, she gave him physical comfort. She didn't think about it as a transaction. She was focused on getting by each day as best she could. If her husband wasn't there to fend for her, she had to take care of herself.

This time she was careful not to get pregnant again. Even though Sui said he would take care of her and her baby if it did happen, she didn't want people to know about their affair. She persuaded Sui to get her mercury, used by prostitutes as a contraceptive.

Although she was trying to be discreet, it was obvious that Sui was spending a lot of time at her house. It wasn't long before word got to his wife, who hadn't been over at the Ma residence since Jade stopped her mother-in-law from hosting mahjong games.

One afternoon, Sui's wife made a surprise visit with her friends. Jade heard the commotion from her bedroom. Sui, who was half-dressed, jumped out of bed and went out by the back door before Jade could even say a word.

'Fox Spirit[6], I can smell your stench from the street. You better come out of your hiding place before I pull you out by your hair. How dare you seduce my husband? He is already an old man. Why don't you find a man of your own age to satisfy your itch?'

Jade couldn't believe Sui ran out on her when she needed him most. She felt so alone. She could hear things being smashed in the house, despite her mother-in-law's attempts to get rid of the intruders.

'What are you doing in my house? I didn't give you permission to come in. I will have you arrested. Help! Help! We are being robbed by bandits!' Madam Ma shouted into the streets.

---

[6] A mischievous spirit who often takes the form of a beautiful woman to seduce men.

Jade steeled her nerves as she got dressed and went out to confront Sui's wife. By then, a crowd had gathered at her front door waiting to see what would happen next. Not even the servants stepped in to help.

'Here's the little whore! You dare to show your face now!'

Jade tried to pacify Sui's wife. 'I'm sure there is some mistake. I don't know what you're talking about … Please calm down. There's no need to make a scene!'

'Calm down? How can I calm down when you stole my husband? He has been spending money on you that should be for our family. If you're afraid of people knowing about your shameful act, you should have more self-respect. Such a disgrace for the Mas to have you as a daughter-in-law!'

Then the crowd stirred. Someone shouted, 'Here's the cheating husband who was trying to run away!'

Sui was being shoved forward by his neighbours and was unable to escape.

Another person shouted, 'Drown the adulterous dog and the bitch in pig baskets[7]!'

Jade was terrified. She didn't know what to do; she had been caught red-handed. It was fortunate Madam Ma couldn't make sense of what was going on.

'Stop this nonsense! We should not be practicing such feudal customs. The couple will have to face the court of law – this is not a circus! Go back to your own homes.' It was one of the town's elders who stepped in to restore order.

As Jade and Sui were dragged to the court house, Sui's wife yelled, 'I'm not going to let you off so easily, you unfaithful bastard!'

She lunged at Sui with a knife before anyone could react. Everyone screamed and ran away in all directions to avoid the crazed woman. It was pandemonium.

---

[7] In the old days, Chinese used to drown adulterous couples in 'Zhu Long' (猪笼 pig baskets) made of bamboo.

It took two brave men to overcome her. She still held on to the knife, now dripping with blood. Sui cried in agony as he lay in the pool of blood that seeped from his crotch.

All the while Sui's wife laughed hysterically. 'Let's see how you can play with women now!'

Jade was in shock. She hid behind her captors for fear that Sui's wife would turn on her too. With the turn of events, Jade was released and it was Sui's wife who was taken to the village jail for castrating her husband. Sui was seriously injured but survived without his manhood.

Jade could not go about her normal life now that her extramarital affair had been exposed. She had lost her financial backer and everyone saw her as a husband-snatcher, no better than a whore.

'I should have known better than to jump into bed with Sui,' Jade thought to herself. 'He's as useless as Tong and as dishonest as Long. It's all because of Long that I had to marry Tong and become a virtual widow. And now this ...'

Madam Ma had forgotten the commotion by the time Jade got back to the house but the relatives were there, demanding that Jade should leave. They felt she had taken advantage of her mother-in-law and had no right to manage the Ma's household, since she was unfaithful to Tong.

'You are a woman of loose morals. We don't want you in our family or our village. Go back to your hometown!'

Jade begged to stay, but the elders refused. As she was about to walk out, her mother-in-law stopped her from leaving.

'Where are you going? Why are these strangers in my house? Don't leave me alone with them!'

Her relatives tried to prevent her from clinging on to Jade, but she fought them tooth and nail.

'You are bad people. Why are you chasing my daughter-in-law away? I will tell my son when he comes home!' Madam Ma was in tears.

'Aren't you ashamed of yourself? See how well your mother-in-law treats you while you drag the Ma's family reputation in the mud!'

The relatives decided to give in to Madam Ma's frantic pleas and let the matter rest for the day. Once they left, Jade collapsed by her mother-in-law's side and cried on her shoulders.

'Mother, I'm so sorry. I have let you down. What are we going to do now? Why isn't Tong here to help us?'

Since her marriage, Jade hadn't kept regular contact with her parents and visited them only once a year, during the Lunar Festival. She was still angry that they didn't support her relationship with Long, but they were the only ones who could possibly help her now.

No one wanted to give them credit at the marketplace and all the servants had left because they didn't want to work for Jade. She was unable to collect any rent from the tenant farmers and had even run out of valuables to pawn.

Jade was not particularly religious compared to her mother, but nonetheless she never failed to visit the temple on the first and fifteenth day of each lunar month to pray to the ancestors for wealth and the well-being of her family members. With the recent events, she was at a loss as what to do. She turned to the gods for guidance.

At the temple, she consulted an oracle. She drew a fortune stick[8] that predicted a change in luck for the better – she was going on a journey. Jade left the temple in a positive frame of mind. 'My husband is coming for me at last!' she thought.

Then another week went by with no news from Tong. Jade thought it was time to swallow her pride and ask her parents for a handout when Mr Cao, her husband's business acquaintance, paid her a surprise visit.

---

[8] Fortune sticks or divinity sticks are used to tell fortunes in Chinese temples. A devotee shakes a container holding the numbered bamboo sticks with both hands while kneeling before the altar until one stick drops out. The stick is taken to a fortune teller, who interprets the corresponding text.

It was the news she was waiting for. Jade ushered the visitor into her house for fear neighbours might expose her infidelity. Mr Cao told Jade that Tong had entrusted him to visit his mother and inform his wife that he had raised enough money for her to join him in America.

'I've been writing to him for months. Do you know why he didn't bother to reply? I thought he was dead! We have suffered hard times in the recent years. He didn't send money like he promised.'

'The shipping lines have been affected because of the Great Depression, which is why he couldn't send money regularly. You don't have to worry any more. He gave me money to help settle any outstanding debts and make your travel arrangements to America. Although he misses his mother, he thinks she is too old and frail to make the long trip and has asked his relative in the countryside to take care of her after you leave.'

Jade stared at the stacks of foreign notes that Mr Cao took out of his briefcase. 'Is that American money from Tong?'

'Yes. He gave me one thousand US dollars to change into Chinese *yuan* at the *jinshanzhuang* so you can pay off your debtors. Tong's business is doing well but he needs more capital to expand, so I've offered to buy this house for cash. Here's a letter from his lawyer in America and a translation of the letter authorising the sale. All I need is your mother-in-law's stamp and the house deeds – I'll take care of the rest and transfer money to the bank. Tong has set up a joint account for you. You are going to be a rich woman!'

'The heavens have eyes! They have answered my prayers. I don't need to put up with people who have laughed behind my back about my absentee Gold Mountain husband. I will tell everyone that my husband has sent for me and invite them to a farewell banquet so they know we still have money!'

'I'm afraid that won't be possible. I have booked you on the next ship to America, leaving tomorrow. The shipping schedules are sporadic so you may have to wait a month or two if you miss this ship – I'm sure you don't want to keep your husband waiting!'

'That seems such a rush ... What about the house sale and our belongings? Not to mention packing for the trip.'

'Don't worry about clothes. Tong will buy you a new wardrobe when you get there. As for the house, I will buy it with all its contents. Tong has instructed me to move the ancestral tablets to the Ma family temple, with a generous donation so they will be cared for. You can write to your family when you arrive in America. You will see them again when Tong comes back with you.'

'What about travel documents? Will I be allowed into America?'

'I have prepared all the necessary documents. I will not be travelling back with you, as I have to finish off the details of the house sale. My associate Mr Lam will meet you on the ship tomorrow – he will coach you on how to answer the questions from the American immigration officers when you arrive.'

'It sounds like you have everything planned ...'

'You can put your mind at ease. You can pack and I will meet you back here tomorrow at noon.'

When Mr Cao left, Jade immediately broke the news to Madam Ma.

'Mother, Tong is still alive! He hasn't abandoned us!'

Madam Ma's face lit up. 'Where is he? Has he returned home? I want to see him now!'

Jade realised it was a bad idea to get Madam Ma excited.

'He's still in America. He wants to come back but he needs more time. I'm going there to help him with his business. With an extra pair of hands, perhaps he can come back sooner.'

'I am getting old. I may not be around when he comes back. Now you are leaving me too ... I have nothing to live for!' Madam Ma sobbed hysterically.

'Don't worry, Mother. We won't forget you. Tong has arranged for someone to take care of you when I leave.'

'I want my son. Where is he?'

It was impossible for Jade to calm her mother-in-law down. Madam Ma finally cried herself to sleep.

Jade had a restless night. On one hand, she was worried about her mother-in-law. On the other, she was excited about her new life in America. All kinds of thoughts were racing through her head.

'I hope Mother won't try to kill herself after I leave ... I don't even know which relative is coming to take care of her. What if they abuse her? I should have asked Mr Cao. I'm sure Tong has planned this carefully. I should trust him. I wonder if we're going to get along, it's hard to read his personality through his letters ... I am going to be boss lady! I wonder if he has any white customers, I need to learn English. Maybe Tong has a car and we can drive around town. I want to watch Western theatre and swim in the ocean.'

Jade tossed and turned all night.

First thing that morning, Jade made an offering at the temple to thank the gods for answering her prayers and for her mother-in-law's health. Back home, Madam Ma seemed to have forgotten what was going on.

'Maybe it's better if I don't remind her that I'm going away,' Jade thought to herself.

She could not bear to see her mother-in-law worked up again. Although Jade felt Madam Ma had been a burden of late, she sincerely cared about her. After all, she was family.

Before leaving with Mr Cao for the port, she made sure her neighbours knew she was going to America. She was disgraced when her affair with Ah Sui came to light. She had to endure harsh looks and insults wherever she went. Finally, she could lift her head up high. To her husband, she was still his honourable wife.

With happy thoughts of a new life ahead, Jade joined her escort Mr Lam on board the ship that would take her to America.

* * *

Jade grew suspicious as soon as she was aboard. She did not get first-class accommodation as Mr Cao promised.

'Why am I not in first class? Surely my husband can afford more than just a bamboo mat on the main deck?' Jade questioned Mr Lam as she shifted her aching bottom on the hard wooden floor.

'Don't worry. You will get first-class passage when we transfer to a bigger ship in Canton. This ferry is too small to withstand the big waves on the open ocean.'

The bad weather appeared to prove his point. Heavy rain caused the river to swell and strong winds tossed the ferry from side to side. With each rocking motion, Jade threw up over the side of the boat. Soon she emptied out all her stomach contents and was left with dry heaves and bile. She was so worn out that she threw up on her bamboo mat and lay there, motionless.

Mr Lam was one of the few people who wasn't overcome by seasickness. He took advantage of Jade as he cleaned her up. Jade was shocked and disgusted, but was too scared to confront him as she was depending on him to take her to America. She dreaded the long journey ahead.

Jade was relieved when the ferry finally docked. There was a hustle and bustle of activity, even though it was just daybreak. Merchant ships were anchored in the harbour. Coolies were loading and unloading goods from junks and sampans closer to shore.

Mr Lam told her to get on a sampan next to their boat. It would transport them to the ship going to America. Jade did not see any reason to panic until they pulled up next to a highly decorated boat with colourful banners. She had heard about these 'flower boats'[9] and knew she had been duped. They were

---

[9] Flower boats were floating brothels that provided sex services to the foreign and Chinese men in the harbour.

not headed for America. She has been sold to a brothel ... a fate worse than death.

'Take me back to the ferry. I am not going in there!' Jade protested.

'Shut up – you don't have a choice!' Mr Lam lunged towards her.

Before he could grab her, Jade decided to take her chances and escape while she could.

Even though she couldn't swim, Jade dived into the water. She tried to hold her breath and kick towards the surface for air. It was pure agony as Jade suffocated from the water rushing into her nose and throat. Soon the lights on the surface faded into darkness as she sank into the murky depths of the Pearl River. As she waited for the river spirits to claim her soul, she prayed for a better fate in her next life.

Jade didn't expect to wake up in bed after that painful ordeal. Her lungs hurt and all the muscles on her body ached when she moved. Judging from the decoration in the room, her attempt had been in vain. She was on the flower boat.

Before she could get out of bed, a woman in her twenties walked in with some food. 'I see you're up. Don't try anything foolish. It's not worth it. You can call me Ah Fang. Like you, I was brought here against my will. My parents were poor and chose to feed their son and not their daughter. After two years, I've earned enough to buy whatever I want and even send money home to remind my parents of their mistake. Life could be worse, so don't despair! You may not believe me now, but it's a good thing you survived. At least you have a chance to be reborn into a better life instead of being a wandering spirit,' Ah Fang said to Jade while holding her hand. 'We are connected by our fate, we will be like sisters from now on. Come – eat something. You'll feel better.'

Jade didn't say a word but wept uncontrollably for the recent suffering, her unforeseen future, and the kindness of a newfound friend.

*   *   *

At twenty-six, Jade was considered old compared to the other girls in the House of Everlasting Happiness who were between the ages of sixteen to twenty. Ah Fang was the most popular one and her name was advertised prominently on a big red lantern that hung outside the boat. She was known to possess special skills that men paid a lot of money for.

It was rumoured that the flower boat was actually owned by a Hong merchant and was therefore protected from police raids. The madam who ran the establishment was called Mrs So, a famous courtesan in her heyday and possibly the mistress of the Hong merchant. Jade never saw Mr Lam again.

From day one, Mrs So warned Jade against insubordination. 'Your wild antics will not be tolerated. You caused me to lose face by behaving badly but I'll give you a second chance, since you are new. You now belong to the House of Everlasting Happiness and will obey by my rules. If you try to hurt yourself again I will make sure you wish you were dead. On the other hand, Ah Fang will tell you that I'm a very fair person – if you are obedient and the customers like you, you will be rewarded handsomely.'

Mrs So kept a close eye on what was happening on the boat. It was not easy for the girls to have any time alone as Mrs So and her loyal maidservant monitored their every move. At any sign of trouble from the girls or the customers, the thugs guarding the flower boat jumped into action.

Jade gave up any hope of being rescued. No one knew she had been kidnapped. After all, she had bragged to her neighbours that she was going to America. Tong would never forgive her for leaving his mother behind and giving away the house to a stranger.

Ah Fang showed Jade how to take control of her destiny.

'You are blessed with good looks; use that to your advantage. Our patrons are all wealthy traders and government officials.

They are generous with their gifts if you know how to please them,' Ah Fang said with a cheeky smile.

'I don't want to be a prostitute,' Jade sulked.

'No one says you are one. You are providing companionship for some very important people who cannot get it at home. These men come here to conduct after-work business with their peers over drinks and food. I see myself as a business facilitator.'

'That's one way of looking at it. But we still have to sell our bodies, nonetheless,' Jade argued.

'Yes, we are expected to sleep with the customers but you shouldn't give yourself away too easily. Give them enough, but not too much, so that they keep coming back for more.'

'Sounds like you are baiting fish!' Jade laughed.

'I like the big ones!'

Jade was amused by Ah Fang's light-hearted approach to their situation.

Like Ah Fang, she made the most of her circumstances and separated her morals from her actions. By embracing her new life, she was able to find some reprieve.

Jade was careful not to get pregnant; it was an occupational hazard. At the same time, she was worried that she wouldn't have any children to care for her in her old age.

She was twenty-seven when she adopted a ten-year-old girl who had been orphaned during a boat fire. She nicknamed her Little Pig[10] in the hope that the gods would spare her from further misfortunes. Jade took a vow in front of Guan Yin, patron goddess of mothers, to care for the child as she would her own.

'Oh merciful one, please watch over my daughter Little Pig. I promise to take care of her as if she were my own. She is a good girl and deserves to be loved. She will be the child I never had.'

Jade was not allowed to have the girl on the flower boat, so

---

[10] Traditionally, Chinese gave their babies an animal name or a deliberately unattractive name to trick evil spirits into overlooking them.

she paid the chef's wife to look after her along with her own children on the sampan. Jade's perspective on life changed, knowing that she had to be responsible for Little Pig. She had to earn as much money as possible to feed her and send her to school. If Little Pig were educated, she could find decent work and take care of Jade in her old age.

In 1938, Jade's life took another turn. With the rumours of Japanese invasion, wealthy Cantonese families escaped to the countryside. Business at the brothels was badly affected. The girls at the House of Everlasting Happiness were told they had to look for customers on land. The girls went to dancing halls in pairs, chaperoned by the madam who kept a watchful eye and negotiated each transaction.

Even then, the brothel struggled financially and the owner seemed to have disappeared abroad to escape the impending war. Without his deep pockets to pay protection money, the flower boat was constantly raided by police and threatened by Triad members for poaching customers on land. Mrs So was helpless and despondent.

It was during one of these raids that Little Pig was taken away by the police. Jade only found out when she came back to the flower boat at dawn to find the chef's wife in tears.

'Sorry, Mistress Jade! The police came by and talked to the children when I wasn't around. Little Pig told the police that her parents died and she was living with a new mother. The police said her parents are still alive and they could take her to them. Little Pig fell for their lie.'

'It's not your fault … Little Pig is too naïve – she shouldn't trust those men so easily. I have to find her before it's too late!'

It was known that the police often kidnapped young girls and took them to Japanese soldiers who would keep them as 'comfort women', sex slaves to be raped until they died from disease or injury.

Although Little Pig was adopted, Jade treated the girl as her flesh and blood. All she could think of was the safety of her daughter. Jade went to the police station to beg for her return, but her pleas fell on deaf ears.

'We don't know who took your daughter. Stop wasting our time.'

A man in plain clothes followed Jade outside. 'I cannot tell you who is responsible but I can guarantee her safety for 1500 silver *yuan*.'

'I don't have 1500 *yuan* right now. If you give me one week to raise the money, I'll give it to you. I just want to make sure she won't be harmed.'

'I want to help you. Meet me back here in a week. If you don't have the money, she will be sent to the comfort station like the rest.'

Jade didn't trust the man – she didn't trust any man – but she had to come up with the money if there was any chance that she could find Little Pig.

Jade's first thought was to turn to Ah Fang for help. She was not as close to the other girls. Jade and Ah Fang had made a pledge before Guan Yin to take care of each other as real sisters would for life. Surely her sworn sister[11] would lend her money to save Little Pig.

'I really want to help you but I don't have much to spare. I put my money in a tontine[12] and won't have access to the funds till our next bid on the first day of the month. What about your parents? You said they're rich. They may be able to help – you should go to them. I will cover for you.'

'Thank you, Ah Fang. I'll take your advice. I just hope my parents will be happy to see me after all these years and help their granddaughter, even if she's adopted.'

---

[11] Sworn sisterhood refers to a lifelong bond between females who are not blood relatives.

[12] Chinese tontine is a form of investment where members pool their money into a common fund. The member who bids the highest interest rate has access to the funds.

*   *   *

Jade had lost touch with her parents since she arrived at the House of Everlasting Happiness. Like the other girls, she was not allowed any outside communication. Jade thought it was just as well because her father would disown her if he knew she was a prostitute.

On the long boat ride back to her village in Kaiping, Jade concocted a story to explain her disappearance. She would tell her parents that she was supposed to join her husband in America but had an accident on the ferry that caused her to lose her memory. She had been working in Canton as a maid, until she remembered recently who she was.

Jade was taking a gamble going back home to her parents. If they didn't help her she would have used up the little money she had on the boat ride. Whatever the outcome, she had to do her best to find Little Pig. She wasn't going back to the House of Everlasting Happiness.

Jade had been away for nine years. She recognised some of the villagers but avoided making eye contact with anyone in case they wanted to start a conversation. She walked purposefully to her parents' house at the end of the village.

Fond memories of her childhood came back to her as she walked down the familiar alleys but as she neared her childhood home, Jade was shocked at what she saw. It was not the homecoming she had envisiged.

The two red lanterns that hung over the front entrance were tattered and torn. The faded New Year couplets on each side of the door looked like they hadn't been changed for many years. There were tiles missing on the roof and the paper window screens needed replacing.

Her father was a respectable village elder and his peers looked to him as a role model. How could her proud father let their ancestral house become run down?

No servants greeted her as she walked through the front door.

Instead, there were strangers in the courtyard outside the rooms which used to house visiting relatives. Then she heard someone call her name.

'Jade, is that really you? Where have you been? I've been so worried about you! I'd almost given up hope that I would see you before I die ... We have to thank our ancestors for their blessings!'

It was her mother, Mei. She looked thin and frail, but nonetheless overjoyed to see her.

'I'm so sorry you had to worry about me. I had an accident in Canton and couldn't even remember who I was until recently.'

'It must be fated that you came back to me! Come inside my room so we can have more privacy.'

Mei's room looked the same, except the silk bedding had become threadbare and some of the beautiful vases that once decorated the room were noticeably missing.

'Mother, what happened? Where are Father and Da-ma?'

'If only you'd come back sooner ... Your father's health suffered as his business took a downturn. Choy took on his responsibilities at the trading firm but business didn't pick up. After we sold the farm, we started to rent out some of the rooms to bring in additional income. Unfortunately, your father's health worsened last winter and he finally passed on. Da-ma decided to join a nunnery and dedicate her life to serving Buddha. I haven't seen her since. I was wondering when our streak of bad luck would end – then you turned up!'

Jade had a sinking feeling that it was going to be a fruitless journey.

'So much has happened while I was away ... Is Choy still running Father's business?'

'Unfortunately, there is nothing left of your father's business. Your drug addict brother spends all his time and money smoking his life away. He is not interested in working at all. Before your father passed away we found him a wife in the hope that she would rein him in, but your brother kept to his old ways.'

'Where is Choy now?'

'He's probably in the village square idling with other wastrels – if he's not smoking opium.'

Jade didn't bother to tell her mother the real reason she was visiting. As the head of the family, her brother would hold the purse strings. Jade hoped that her close ties with her brother would play to her advantage.

At the centre of the village square was a banyan tree her grandfather had planted when he was a boy. Just as Mei predicted, Choy was under the tree with his friends. Jade couldn't help thinking of the old proverb, 'One generation plants a tree, another gets the shade.' Her grandfather and father had such high hopes for her brother.

Jade could hardly recognise her little brother. He was emaciated and had the tell-tale signs of an opium eater – pale, waxy skin and bluish lips – similar to those Jade had seen with some of her patrons. Even though her mother didn't mention it, Jade suspected that her brother's wayward behaviour may have contributed to her father's early death.

'Choy!' she called.

The men all turned to Choy and teased him about having a mistress. It was obvious that they didn't recognise her.

Choy was startled but happy to see her and greeted his sister with a broad smile.

'I can't believe it's you! After all these years …' Turning to his friends, he said, 'I need to catch up with my sister. See you tomorrow.'

'You've been away for so long! Mother and Father missed you so badly. Have you been home?'

'Yes, I've seen Mother and heard about Father. I wish I'd come back sooner. I suffered amnesia due to an accident on a trip to Canton and have been working there till recently. I forgot who I was and lived a new life – even adopted a daughter. The trauma of my daughter's kidnap jolted my memory.'

'That explains why we didn't hear from you all this time! Someone from your village told Father that you'd left for America. We found that hard to believe because we've had no news from you.'

'I'm sorry I made everyone worry. So much has happened while I was in Canton. I have been back to my village and it seems both my mother-in-law and my husband have passed away, leaving me nothing. To be frank, I'm here because I need your help. I don't want to be a burden on anyone but I need money to get my daughter back. The kidnappers are going to send her away to a comfort station. I can't let that happen!'

'Second Sister, I want to help you, but I don't have the means. Father died with a lot of debt from the failing business. We're renting out the house to get by. We still get rice from our ancestral farms but we have no additional revenue. All the valuables have been sold or pawned.'

Choy painted a bleak picture.

'But I know someone who can help ... Big Sister.'

Jade had never contemplated getting help from Phoenix. She was too proud to ask. Jade held a grudge against her sister for marrying Long; if she had married him, life would have been different. It would have been better.

Even though Phoenix was a girl, she was her father's favourite child. Jade heard that Phoenix received a handsome dowry from her father. It was only fair that she should share that inherited wealth with her siblings.

Before his visit to Phoenix, Choy assured Jade that he would secure the money for rescuing Little Pig.

Jade didn't question Choy's intentions as he had always been faithful to her. She was thankful that he was willing to approach Phoenix for a loan – she wasn't ready to do so herself, however desperate she was.

*　*　*

71

Phoenix didn't expect to see Choy at her home. Although they met at family events and lunar festivals, she never felt Choy was very close to her; perhaps it was down to his relationship with Jade.

It wasn't a surprise when Choy revealed the reason for his visit. Despite the rift with Jade over her marriage to Long years ago, Phoenix still held her close to her heart. She was worried when her parents lost touch with her sister and prayed continually for her safe return. It was a relief to know that Jade was well, but a disappointment that she refused to meet her in person.

Clearly, the past was still not behind them.

'Choy, I would like to help Phoenix but I am now a wife and mother and need to think of my own family.'

'Big Sister, Father was generous to you when he was alive. Now that Second Sister is in need, she is counting on you to do the same. I would help her but I need to pay off Father's debts so we don't lose the roof over our heads.'

'I am thankful for Father's generosity and would gladly help Jade – but why doesn't she come to meet me? I've been worried about her since her disappearance. I hope she's not still holding a grudge against me.'

'I didn't tell Second Sister I'm here. I know you've had a misunderstanding and I want to help mend that relationship by giving you the opportunity to help. She may not accept the money if I tell her it's from you – but once she's saved her daughter, I will tell her the truth and she will be very grateful.'

'I don't expect her to be grateful! All I want is for us to be sisters again. Even though we have different mothers, she's the only sister I have and you are my only brother.'

From under the bed, Phoenix pulled out a jewelry box and inside was a gold bracelet, still bright and shiny despite being hidden for years.

'Father gave me this gold bracelet for my wedding. It's very precious to me but I know Jade needs the money more than I do. Tell her that she will always be my dearest sister.'

5

Wartime Hardships

Phoenix entrusted Choy to pass her gold bracelet to Jade. As part of her dowry, she planned to give it to her future daughter-in-law as a family heirloom. Although she found it hard to part with such a precious gift from her late father, she knew Jade had more immediate need for it. After all, you can't measure family ties in gold.

However, Choy had his own plans for the gold bracelet. When his father died, Choy was left in the lurch with no financial skills, more concerned about opium than running his father's business. The gold bracelet meant instant cash. He could sell it or pawn it, either way he would get his next smoke.

For 300 *yuan*, Choy pledged the bracelet to his friend Fung whose father owned a pawn shop. Fung was not willing to buy it for more but Choy was not discouraged. The bracelet didn't belong to him anyway; it was money from the heavens.

With the money in his pocket, Choy went back to Jade with a shameless lie.

'Second Sister, I have talked to Big Sister and she has let us down. She said that as a married woman, her family is her immediate concern. She will not help you, despite my pleas.'

'I knew she was selfish! I was prepared to forgive her and yet she turned her back on me again! It goes to show blood is not thicker than water. She's not my sister – I disown her. I will have to come up with the money some other way.'

'I would lend you money ... but we can hardly scrape by with the rent we're getting.'

Choy was not concerned about saving Jade's adopted daughter, since she was not a blood relative. He told his wife that the girl was better off dead. Ah Lan didn't want to question her husband's judgment. She was Tanka and had lived on a boat all her life; she knew little about the life of people on shore until she was married into the Wong household.

Ah Lan was the oldest daughter. Her mother wanted her to marry into a Tanka family, but her father was enticed by the dowry that Wong's matchmaker offered. He had nine children; to him, it meant one less mouth to feed.

On her wedding day, Ah Lan received a jade bracelet from her mother-in-law, Mei. It was the most valuable thing she had ever owned. She believed the gemstone had powers to protect the wearer and wore it proudly from her wedding day, until a terrible experience with Choy.

'Ah Lan, that's a pretty bracelet. Why don't you take it off so I can admire it?'

'I've worn this since our wedding day. Why do you want to look at it now?' Ah Lan was surprised by the strange request. Choy hardly paid any attention to her.

'I can get you a nicer one.'

'This is a present from your mother. I don't need a nicer one.' Ah Lan grew suspicious and subconsciously touched her bracelet.

'You say it's a present from my mother, so why are you trying to hide it from me?' Choy's mood turned sour. He grabbed her wrist in an attempt to pull the bracelet off.

'Please stop, you're hurting me!' Ah Lan cried in pain as she tried to pull away from him.

'I want the bracelet. Don't make me chop off your hand to get it,' Choy threatened.

Ah Lan managed to get away from him, slamming her wrist against the side of a table in the process. The bracelet broke in half but saved Ah Lan's wrist from the impact.

'Look what you've done, you stupid woman! I needed that bracelet to buy my opium.' Choy was furious that he had ended up with two halves of a jade bracelet that he couldn't get any money for.

'You think you look so pretty with that bracelet, don't you? I will teach you a lesson for being so vain.'

Choy proceeded to beat her up, despite her desperate pleas.

Hidden by her clothes, the bruises on her arms and legs were reminders of his fiery temper. Even though Ah Lan knew it was not right for Choy to take Phoenix's bracelet, she was not about to challenge him.

All she could do was offer a prayer to the Wong ancestors for the safety of the little girl.

Jade went back to Canton, oblivious to her brother's betrayal. Her mother tried to persuade her to stay for her own safety, but Jade said she had unfinished business. She knew what she had to do. She would offer herself to the Japanese soldiers in return for her daughter. There was no other way.

In a matter of days, Canton was in a state of chaos as the Japanese soldiers became more active and aggressive. The British forces were not able to maintain control over the city. There were few buses going to Canton while refugees continued flooding out. Jade got as far as Foshan on a coal-fired bus, but was told she needed a permit of transit issued by the Imperial Japanese Army Headquarters for South China to get into Canton.

Jade continued on foot. She was determined that her daughter would not suffer her fate. It was a slow trek and she was going against the flow; thousands were fleeing the city for the safety of the countryside. The sick and the injured found no respite from the summer heat. Families carried their belongings on their backs. The lucky ones loaded their donkeys and hand carts with straw mats and cooking pots, alongside their children and the elderly.

Jade was starving. She didn't have any belongings that she could trade for food and couldn't bring herself to beg. She noticed people were foraging for wild vegetables and sweet potatoes by the roadside and did likewise. There was a family of four cooking on an open fire under a tree; she offered to throw in her sweet potatoes and vegetables in the pot if she could have some of their *congee*.

'Thank you for sharing your food. May Buddha bless you on your journey.'

'Don't mention it. In these times, we need to stand united. If you don't mind me asking, where is your family?' asked the father.

'I'm going back to Canton to get my daughter. The police took her away ... possibly for the Japanese soldiers. I don't know whether she's dead or alive.' Jade broke down in tears as she confronted the harsh reality of the situation.

'I'm sorry to hear that. I don't know what I would do if something happened to my family,' said the mother, as she gathered her arms around her two children.

'Canton is not a city to be in now. There is death and destruction everywhere, the city's still burning from the air raids. We're heading to our ancestral home outside of Shunde for refuge. The Japanese are focused on invading the major cities, not the small villages – you would be safer in the countryside, too.'

'Thank you for your concern. No matter what, I have to save my daughter first. She doesn't have anyone else except me.'

Jade continued her journey; it was nightfall before she arrived on the outskirts of Canton where Japanese soldiers had erected checkpoints. She saw soldiers standing on guard to inspect everyone going in and out. Communication was going to be a problem as she didn't speak any Japanese.

She stood in line and steadied herself as she waited her turn. As she approached the guard, she bowed as low as she could. She heard from some of the refugees that people were beaten up badly if the Japanese soldiers didn't feel they were respected.

'I need to get into Canton. My daughter is still in the city. I need to find her – please help me,' Jade pleaded.

'Transit permit! Transit permit!' the Japanese guard barked in strongly accented Cantonese, waving a piece of paper.

Jade refused to be turned away. The guard shouted at her and brandished his rifle. Jade didn't understand a word but from his body language, he clearly wanted her to stop. The commotion attracted the attention of the other guards.

The guard reacted by beating Jade with the butt of his rifle. Jade fell to her knees and tried to deflect the blows with her arms, but each one found her skin and bones. She curled up in a ball from the pain while the bystanders looked on.

Suddenly she felt someone shielding her, using their body to protect her from the assault. It was a Western lady in a white gown with a hood … It was a nun. The gesture surprised the guard so much so that he stopped his brutal attack on Jade, now semi-conscious from her injuries.

The nun, whom Jade came to know as Sister Marie, was one of the many standing in line to get back into the city. Speaking in English, she offered a couple of bottles of wine in exchange for Jade. The guard felt it was a good enough bargain and allowed her to leave with Sister Marie.

She was back in Canton at last.

Jade was relieved that she was not surrounded by Japanese soldiers when she woke up in a room with rows of army cots.

'Where am I?' she asked the Chinese nun standing beside her bed. She winced from the pain of her injuries; severe bruising on her face, ribs, arms and legs, barely being able to see through her swollen eyes.

'You're in St Vincent's Orphanage in Canton. I am Sister Margaret. Sister Marie brought you here. You've been unconscious for two days now – I'm glad you're feeling better. I'll go and tell Sister Marie that you're awake, she's been taking care of you day and night!' Sister Margaret rambled excitedly before she ran outdoors.

Jade looked out through the window closest to her bed and saw Sister Margaret approach another nun who seemed to be supervising a gardening project in the courtyard. Jade recognised the tall Western woman who had shielded her during the attack.

'How are you feeling, my child?' As she sat down beside her on the bed, Sister Marie surprised Jade by speaking to her in almost perfect Cantonese.

'I am feeling much better. Thank you for saving my life.'

'I'm glad I could help. I was at the right place at the right time. I had just visited the house of a parishioner who donated his food and wine to the orphanage before going back to England. I wasn't sure if the soldier would take the bottles, but he did. God works in strange ways.'

'I don't know how to repay you. If it wasn't for you, I wouldn't be able to get back into the city to find my daughter.'

'I heard you telling the guard that before he started beating you senseless. I'm sorry about your daughter's plight – I will pray for her. You're welcome to stay with us for as long as you like. For now, just save your energy and get better, have some *congee*. I'm afraid we have limited food supplies, we try to supplement our rice rations by growing our own vegetables. It is not much but we're happy to share with those who are in need.'

Jade found out later that the orphanage was converted into a refugee camp, like many others set up by religious groups for Chinese people who were uprooted by the war. Since the orphanage was run by British nuns, it was tolerated by the Japanese army.

A small plot of land in the courtyard of the house was cleared for growing vegetables to be bartered for rice and other necessities. Water mains were destroyed during the air raids, so water from the well had to be rationed. All the adults were assigned chores to keep the refugee camp running while the children took lessons from the nuns during the day. Jade was thankful that Sister Marie had taken her in, even though she would be an extra mouth to feed and another demand on the meagre medical supplies.

The orphanage had previously housed 100 children; some were just babies. The building survived the air raids with little damage while many homes around it were completely destroyed. Homeless families started appearing on Sister Marie's doorstep, seeking food and shelter. She turned to the orphanage's affiliated church in England and benefactors to send aid, so she could feed everyone and 'do God's work'.

In order to house the new residents, the nuns rearranged the living quarters so women and children were in one dormitory, while the men were in another. Some of these refugees enjoyed a privileged lifestyle before the Japanese invasion but lost everything when their homes were destroyed. Others were migrant workers from rural regions who did not have the means to get back home.

War was an equaliser. No one was spared. Everyone Jade spoke to had lost friends and loved ones. Some had died while others were missing, like her daughter. The city continued to burn in some areas. On certain days, Jade smelled the stench of death and rotting flesh in the air. She was worried about Little Pig being alone out there, but couldn't do anything about it.

It wasn't safe for civilians, especially women, to be seen outdoors. Japanese soldiers were everywhere and easily provoked to violence. Some Chinese collaborated with the Japanese and were allowed to move about freely. They were despised, regarded as 'running dogs' for the enemy. Mr Tsang was one of these traitors, who frequently visited his mother at the refugee camp.

'Mr Tsang, I need your help,' Jade approached him discreetly.

'My mother told me you needed information about a missing person.'

'My daughter Little Pig was kidnapped a month ago. I suspect she's been taken to the Japanese. How can I confirm her whereabouts and save her?'

'I'm afraid this would be an impossible task. The Japanese have converted local hotels and buildings to "comfort houses" that are guarded by soldiers – women taken to these comfort houses are given fake identities, no one goes by their real name. They are not supposed to exist. I advise you to give up looking.'

Jade was devastated.

Some thought that Chinese peasants in the countryside fared better than the city folk during the Japanese invasion, since they had better access to food and protection from the Communist Red Army guerrillas. From Phoenix's experience, Japanese atrocities were as rampant in the rural areas as they were in the cities.

Phoenix lived in daily fear for her family's safety. One step out of line and it could be their last. In a neighbouring village, one man refused to give up his chickens to the Japanese so the soldiers tied him up and made him watch them rape his mother, wife and daughter before killing the entire family with their bayonets. Phoenix and the other women hid in nearby hills with their children whenever the soldiers came close to the village.

The men were helpless against the ruthless Japanese soldiers. Long stood by when soldiers raided his ancestral home and took everything of value but Phoenix was shocked when he wanted to join the local resistance forces.

'We have to fight back. The Japanese have robbed us of our wealth, dignity and freedom. We can't just sit here and take the insults. Teacher Deng says my assignment will be very safe – I just need to deliver messages and pass orders. Since I'm a teacher and farmer, the soldiers wouldn't suspect that I have anything to do with the guerrillas.'

Despite toiling endless hours in the rice fields to feed his family, Long still looked like a demure school teacher who was no more capable of holding a gun than he would be a hoe.

'Why does it have to be you? There are other men in the village that can do the job. What if Teacher Deng is wrong? Can he give me my husband back?'

'If I don't join the guerrillas, we won't get their protection – we'll be as good as dead. The guerrillas are better armed and funded than the invading forces so it makes sense to give them our support.'

Phoenix put her foot down and said, 'You're the head of this household. We cannot survive without you. Let's not fight about it!'

She wondered if she made the right decision to give her gold bracelet to Jade. It was uncertain how long the Japanese invasion would last. What if her family needed to escape? She didn't have enough money to pay the traffickers to smuggle them into British-ruled Hong Kong. She should have prioritised her own family's needs above her sister's.

Phoenix would have stuck to her decision not to let Long join the guerrillas if not for her daughter, Jing Jing. She was an intelligent three-year-old who could recite Tang poetry and babysit her little brother. Even as an infant, Jing Jing was advanced for her age; she could walk and talk by the age of six months.

Jing Jing was a loving sister to her baby brother Kyong Kyong. Their names were chosen by Long, since they were born after Long's father passed away. Following the Cheng family tradition, children took their first name from the rhyming couplet that hung over the family's ancestral altar. Each generation had a different character so family members could identify their peers. Jing Jing and Kyong Kyong's name started with Min, meaning 'scholarly'.

Jing Jing was growing up in a generation of change. Phoenix had high hopes for both her son and daughter, but with the onset of the Japanese occupation it was uncertain what the future held.

As rumours of the Japanese invasion spread, families pulled their children out of schools all around the country. 'Will you be able to find another job?' Phoenix asked when Long said that classes were suspended and the schools were shutting.

'There won't be any teaching jobs for sure, but not to worry. We can live very simply, I'll work on our farms to feed the family.' Long put on a brave front, but he had never worked on the farm in his whole life.

'Our tenant farmers can't afford to pay the rent and are working only for food. I don't think they would be happy to see you taking a bigger share.' Phoenix wasn't so sure the plan would work.

'They have no choice. It's my land. They can leave if they find another landowner as generous as I am. Anyway, I'm sure I can increase production if I work on the rice fields.'

'Well, there is certainly a demand for rice on the black market so if we can produce more, we can feed the family and I can use the extra to trade for basic goods.'

Phoenix had little to worry about while Long had the farm, which was why she was adamant that he didn't risk his life by joining the guerrillas. At least, that was what she thought.

She did not expect that Jing Jing would fall sick and need medical attention. Since the Japanese soldiers started appearing around the village, women hid at home with their children. Jing Jing mysteriously fell ill one day with flu symptoms, even though she had little contact with other children. It was rumoured that the Japanese had released biological weapons to sicken the Chinese.

Phoenix turned to traditional remedies when Jing Jing broke out in a fever. She rolled a hard-boiled egg over her forehead to bring her temperature down and made her drink barley water, but to no avail. Phoenix was at a loss. There were no doctors in the village.

Teacher Deng heard about the situation and offered help from the guerrillas, who had a medic. 'Comrade Sister, I know Jing

Jing is very sick. If you don't mind, I have access to Western medicine that can help her get better right away.'

'Thank you for your concern, Teacher Deng. My daughter is already taking Chinese medicine. I fear Western medicine may do more harm than good. I am grateful for your offer to help nonetheless.'

'Hear the man out. He may be able to save our daughter's life!' Long was keen to try all options.

'Comrade Sister, I don't want to interfere with how you care for your child. I personally believe in our traditional medicine but Jing Jing is now beyond that. I have seen similar cases before. She needs an extra boost to get better.'

'We shouldn't be biased against Western medicine, just because we don't know it. We should keep our minds open.'

'You're right. We have tried everything within our means. If Teacher Deng has seen it work with others, then it may work for Jing Jing.'

Phoenix felt indebted to Teacher Deng when Jing Jing recovered after several doses of aspirin.

'I know the guerillas have a limited medical supply and yet you were willing to offer help to my daughter. I am eternally grateful.'

'Jing Jing is the generation we're fighting for. I want Jing Jing and all our children to grow up strong and be our future leaders in a world free of oppression.'

'I'm beginning to understand your point of view. I was hesitant when Long first said he wanted to join you, but now I totally support his decision. I trust you'll take care of him.'

'I am happy that you've come around. Long is a good man. Don't worry, I'll take care of him.'

After Long joined the guerrillas, Phoenix found out that many other villagers were also actively involved. Farmers contributed by raising livestock; other educated men like Long helped to communicate with the occupied cities. There were also women in the resistance. Siu Ma was one of them.

She was the medic who cured Jing Jing, brought by Teacher Deng to Phoenix's house when he found out that the child was sick. Siu Ma was a nurse who joined the resistance forces to avenge her family members, killed by the Japanese. When they met, she told Phoenix that Jing Jing reminded her of her own daughter.

'My daughter died when the Japanese invaded my parents' village. I was widowed at a young age and my daughter was all I had. She lived with her grandparents while I worked in the city hospital. They are all dead now and I'm alone, so I decided to fight the Japanese. After all, I have nothing to lose.'

'You're very brave. I don't think I could do what you do – it's hard to be on the road travelling from one village to the next.'

'Our team has been successful in ambushing Japanese soldiers and traitors. We're slowly chipping away at their defense, but we need to carry on so we can overthrow their control.'

Phoenix wondered whether it was fate that Jing Jing fell sick, resulting in her friendship with Siu Ma, the unwavering supporter of the resistance forces.

As Teacher Deng promised, Long had a relatively safe role as a messenger for the guerrillas. There were resistance forces in all the neighbouring villages. It was difficult to coordinate movements without passing information to each other.

At night, the guerrillas in Long's village hid messages and maps in a woven basket, stored in his shed. During the day Long took the basket to his farm, which bordered the neighbouring village. He left the notes at a designated spot where they were picked up under the cover of darkness. Even though he sometimes passed Japanese soldiers on his way, they never suspected him.

He didn't get paid, as the resistance forces were mostly civilian volunteers. Occasionally the guerrillas would leave him a basket of eggs or a bottle of rice wine that he could then barter for other essentials. One day, he was surprised to find a man lying face down on the dry hay in the shed.

With shovel in hand, he prodded the man and shouted, 'What are you doing here?'

The man was startled from his sleep. 'Please don't hurt me! We're on the same side ... I'm with the Guangzhou guerrilla force. My name is Kong – my brother and I were exposed by a traitor in our village. The Japanese caught my brother Ming, but I managed to escape. I used to deliver messages here so I know this is a safe house.'

Long recognised Kong as he moved into the light. 'Cheng Kong – I know you. We are distant cousins descended from the same great grandfather, but now we are brothers with a common cause. I would invite you into my house, but I have a family to protect, so it's best that you stay here.'

'Thank you for giving me shelter, I'll make my way across the border to Hong Kong after dark, but I would like to ask you for a favour. I know where they've taken my brother and I can't leave without knowing if he's safe. We were taken to an abandoned house with other suspected guerrillas – it's in a field by the river that runs past your village. Can you see if he's there?'

'I want to help, but you're asking a lot. What if the Japanese are still there?'

'You look like a gentle farmer. If you meet any of the soldiers just bow to them, don't look them in the eye. I will be forever grateful!'

Long agreed to help Kong and without losing precious time, he made his way to the abandoned house. He knew exactly where to look; it was in the field where he used to secretly meet Jade.

He had his farmer's hat on and made a show of picking wild vegetables in case he ran into any soldiers. Long's heart raced as he came close to the house. He was taking an unnecessary risk to help his fellow clansman. What if the Japanese soldiers found him? He had no doubt that he would be shot.

From outside, the house looked idyllic. Inside was a different story. When Long peeked in the tattered window pane, there was a pile of motionless bodies in the corner. They were freshly dead and instead of the smell of death, there was a smell of fear. The floor was wet with a mixture of vomit, urine and faeces.

Long could not believe what he was looking at. He has seen dead people but this was different. These men had been tortured to death. There was no way Ming would still be alive.

He took a bold step into the house and called Ming's name. He didn't expect a reply but heard a groan; someone was alive in the pile of corpses.

'Ming?'

'Help me ...'

It was a miracle. Ming was alive. Long quickly pulled him free from the dead bodies. He looked relieved to be rescued. Ming's naked chest bore the imprints of boots[13]. He clearly had been stamped on after being pumped full of water and left to die. Long checked each of the bodies in case any of the others were still alive.

Ming was very weak, but Long forced him onto his feet.

'I have to get you away from here! The Japanese soldiers might come back. They'll kill both of us if we are still here. We can take the path along the river back to the village. Your brother Kong is hiding in the safehouse.'

With much difficulty, Ming stumbled along with his arm on Long's shoulder. Now and then he coughed up water and blood.

'You're my saviour. I owe you my life!'

'We're blood brothers. You have risked your life to fight the Japanese. It's only right that I do my part.'

Kong was overjoyed that his brother was still alive. He asked Long to inform the local guerrilla leader that they were both on the run and in need of medication.

---

[13] Water treatment was a common form of torture used by the Japanese during the Second World War. The victim was bound and water was forced via the mouth and nostrils to the lungs and stomach, until he lost consciousness. Pressure was then applied by jumping on the stomach to force the water out.

Teacher Deng offered assistance in getting them to the border of Hong Kong.

While Ming was on the mend, Long came to hear about the brothers' activities. They were both very good oarsmen and often spied on a Japanese camp along the river. On one of their night missions, Kong shot a Japanese soldier who was urinating by the embankment. The gunshot alerted other soldiers to intruders but the brothers managed to sail away unnoticed – or so they thought.

A neighbour in the village was fishing on the river and saw the two brothers get away. He was a young man with a lot of anger towards the Kuomintang as his father had joined the army, leaving him and his mother to fend for themselves. He went to the Japanese as a witness of the murder of the soldier in return for benefits.

Even before they were found out, Kong was having nightmares about the soldier whom he killed. Although he felt brave for killing the enemy, he was guilty of taking a man's life. When Ming was captured, Kong burnt a cigarette and poured rice wine on the ground as offerings to the spirit of the dead man for fear it was seeking revenge.

Having found his brother alive and well, Kong made immediate plans to leave the fighting behind and escape to Hong Kong, where they had family.

Phoenix was unhappy that Long had put his life in danger by rescuing Ming. 'I don't understand why you put yourself at risk like that. You told me that you would be careful. Even if you don't care about me, you need to think about your children. Do you want them to grow up without a father?' Phoenix was deeply agitated.

'This is part of what I signed up for as a resistance fighter! Ming risked his life for the cause. It is only right that I should try do my best,' Long insisted.

'I regret the day you joined the resistance. Have you ever

considered this rescue mission might draw unnecessary attention to you or to our family? Or doesn't it matter?'

'It's not like I am telling everyone. If I keep quiet, no one will know.'

'I hope that's the case.' But Phoenix had her doubts.

True to form, Long revelled in his new status as a hero and embellished his story in front of friends and family.

'There were Japanese lurking everywhere. I had to be careful not to attract their attention. Every move I made was a calculated risk. I pretended to be collecting wild vegetables in the field and as I bent down to pick the plants, I looked around from under my straw hat to make sure I wasn't being followed. I could hear distant gunshots and birds flying into the air. They were close ... And then I saw the house Kong told me about. I told myself I had to be brave for the sake of our fellow comrades. I could hear my heart pounding, but I had to remain calm. I was outraged by what I saw in the house. Corpses everywhere. Those Japanese soldiers have no respect for the dead ... I offered a quick prayer to them. I couldn't save them and needed to focus on finding those alive. I had to act quickly in case the Japanese came back. I heard a sound coming from a stack of dead bodies – and it was Ming.

'He was barely alive from the water treatment and left for dead. He would have died if I hadn't rescued him in time! He was pinned under the dead bodies and didn't have the strength to free himself. He was hurt very badly so I carried him back here. It was a terrifying experience but I would do it all over again!'

Phoenix was tired of hearing this story. She worried about Long getting himself into trouble and risking the safety of their family. She needed an escape route and just like the Cheng brothers Kong and Ming, Phoenix wanted the family to flee to Hong Kong but was worried about how they would support themselves once they were there.

'Siu Ma, I'm worried for my children. They're so young and

it's just too dangerous here. The Japanese forces are killing men, women and children indiscriminately. I would take them to Hong Kong if I had the money.'

'Sister Phoenix, you have to support your husband. Everyone has to do their part for the anti-Japanese effort. If we stand united, we will win the war! You should join us in our fight against the Japanese. You can control your destiny and your children's future by standing alongside your husband, it will help take your mind off negative thoughts. I know you're good at sewing – perhaps you could make shoes for the men? They're always on the move and their shoes get worn out easily. Since their womenfolk are not around to help with mending, they would be grateful if you could take care of their feet. You could get paid and start saving up for your big escape.'

'Yes, I will help. I hope one day my children will be proud that I did my part to defend the country.'

Phoenix made used of her needlework skills to make shoes and mend uniforms for the predominantly male resistance forces. In return, Siu Ma – who was the intermediary – gave Phoenix rice and coal that she then traded for black market silver. Little did she realise that this would come back to haunt her after the war.

Life in Canton was unpredictable. Jade had been at the orphanage for a year before giving up all hopes of finding her daughter alive; no one had ever heard of a comfort woman escaping from the Japanese. Even though Sister Marie was a devout Catholic, she didn't encourage Jade to believe in miracles.

It was a very difficult task for Sister Marie as a white woman to maintain her own safety and that of the residents. According to Sister Margaret, Sister Marie came from a wealthy background and devoted herself to God at an early age.

One day, Jade asked her why she didn't leave when she had a chance.

'This is my family. How can I leave my family?'

Jade reflected on the state of her own family. She had disowned Phoenix as a sister. Little Pig was now lost to her. She felt sorry for herself. She often confided in Mr Tsang, as he knew about Little Pig.

Most people avoided talking to him because he was seen as a Japanese collaborator. He didn't work directly for the Japanese army but was a clerk at a Japanese trading company that was still operating during the occupation. Because of his connections, he was able to provide necessities to his mother (and so indirectly to the orphanage) that were scarce in wartime.

Mr Tsang was a good listener and didn't come across as being untrustworthy. Jade started looking forward to his visits, although sometimes he would go weeks without visiting his mother. Even though she told herself not to trust any man, Jade was tempted to think Mr Tsang was different.

She never asked him about work and he never talked about it. Jade knew people looked at them suspiciously when they were chatting alone. She didn't care. They could all be dead tomorrow. At least she was doing something she enjoyed at that moment – sharing a conversation with someone she liked.

Mr Tsang never expressed his feelings for her and Jade didn't want to be presumptuous, so she never said anything either. Whenever they said goodbye, he would say, 'It will be a fine day when we meet again.'

Jade always waited for that fine day.

6

Post War

The Japanese occupation started in 1931, lasting until 1945. During that time, everyone did their best to survive. Some scavenged for food and hid in the hills. Some moved to farms in the countryside. Others remained in the cities, surviving on meagre food rations.

For Jade, the days at the orphanage seemed endless. She was almost happy about being in limbo. Even though she had barely enough to eat, she was no longer a prostitute and felt like she had a purpose in life.

Jade volunteered to take care of the orphans. In a way, she hoped that if she performed good deeds Little Pig would be blessed and not be harmed. Working indoors also meant she could stay out of the sun. The last thing she wanted was to look like a peasant.

Jade didn't feel guilty about being choosy. At least she was earning her keep; some of the refugees were completely idle from one meal to the next. Sister Marie taught English lessons using the Bible to keep these refugees occupied and motivated.

Jade too attended the lessons because she liked the stories about Jesus. Guan Yin had not saved her daughter. Maybe the white man's god would. She heard the story about Jesus and the little girl – how he raised her from the dead – and asked Sister Marie if Jesus would help her find Little Pig if she believed in Him. She said, 'All things are possible if you have faith.'

'Whatever you say, I cannot believe in your god. Otherwise I will be punished. My ancestors will blame me for starving them in hell if I do not burn paper money and offerings for them.'

Jade was not particularly religious, but ultimately she was not prepared to dishonour her ancestors by converting.

When she wasn't caring for the children or attending Bible classes, Jade entertained the others with songs. She used to perform excerpts from Cantonese operas for her patrons. She enjoyed being the centre of attention and revelled in the applause. She thought that perhaps after the war she could become a professional opera singer.

The relatively carefree life at the orphanage didn't last forever. Two years into the Japanese occupation, Sister Marie was forced to close the shelter.

'I'm afraid we have bad news to share.' Sister Marie had gathered everyone in the main hall to make her announcement.

'The Japanese occupying force has ordered all shelters to close down. We have been given one month's supply of food before we have to get out of this building.'

There was commotion all around.

'Where will we go? Our homes have been destroyed!'

'You will have to find a permanent place to live or leave the city. The Japanese will punish anyone who disobeys the orders.'

Jade was afraid to leave. Where would she go? If she went back to her village, she would see Phoenix and Long. The only family she had in Canton was her mother's sister, whom she stayed with when the scandal with Long broke out; she would have to find out if Second Aunty still lived there.

Jade never ventured outside the orphanage for fear of the Japanese. Again, Mr Tsang came to her aid by taking a message to her aunt. The reply told her that the old lady had passed away, but was survived by her uncle and cousins. Her cousins were willing to take Jade in if she could help take care of her bedridden uncle.

'This is a good offer. You're so good with the children, I'm sure you would be a wonderful nurse for your uncle,' Mr Tsang encouraged Jade. 'At least if you stay in the city, I can visit you.'

Jade didn't expect her relationship with Mr Tsang to go anywhere. From her experience, it was better not to have any expectations than to have them dashed. At least it was comforting to know that Mr Tsang still wanted to see her.

She took up the offer from her cousins and left the orphanage.

To her surprise, Jade was readily accepted into the Lau household. She imagined that with the wartime shortages, her arrival meant there was even less to go around. Jade's cousins Wing and Ting – who had led Choy astray – were now both married and had families of their own.

Their wives were not friendly with each other and each pushed their father-in-law's well-being on to the other. Wing's wife was married to the older son while Ting's wife had no children, so each thought it should be the other's responsibility.

In his heyday, Old Lau had a household of servants at his beck and call. The Japanese invasion brought an end to his business; his warehouses by the river were burnt to the ground during the air raids. All that he owned was invested in his business but at least he still had a roof over his head.

He survived the shock of losing his livelihood, but not the shock of his wife's death. He loved her so much that he never took a concubine like other men did. He was happy to spend his life with just one woman. It was the shock of her death that brought on his stroke. He spent his days looking at the ceiling, waiting for the time to come when he could see her again.

He had no patience for his two quarrelsome daughter-in-laws. If he still had money, they would both be fawning over him. Instead they argued about whose turn it was to empty the spittoon[14] or feed him.

The stroke affected his speech and movement but he still had

---

[14] Chinese traditionally kept spittoons in the bedroom to pass urine at night.

a coherent mind. They treated him like he was already dead because he couldn't speak. His sons didn't intervene since it was the women's place, as the caretakers of the family.

The women had another argument the day Jade's letter arrived.

'I don't know about you, but I wish I were deaf. I've had enough of the bickering about Father,' Wing said to his brother.

'There may be a solution in sight. Do you remember our cousin Jade, Choy's sister?'

'Of course I do. She was a pretty girl, I would have dated her if we weren't related. I heard she married a Gold Mountain guest.'

'Your wife would give you even more grief if she heard what you just said. Anyway, Father received a letter from her asking for room and board. She didn't say what happened to her husband, but clearly she's on her own.'

'Maybe I can get my way with her.'

'You're sick. Let's be serious. We need someone other than our wives to take care of Father. She can be that someone.'

'You're right. Timing couldn't be better. We don't need to consult Father. Tell her she is welcome in our home and to come as soon as possible, so we can get some peace and quiet.'

Jade did not care to be dragged into the household politics. Since she had experience taking care of her mother-in-law, she didn't find taking care of Old Lau to be odious – but he was certainly heavier, so it was more physically demanding to bath and change him.

Jade spent more time with Old Lau than his family did. Even though they all lived in the same house, the sons came by only to greet him good morning and good night, whereas Jade slept in a cot in Old Lau's room to make sure he didn't accidentally choke on his saliva. She didn't have to worry about him taking advantage of her, since he was immobile.

*   *   *

Old Lau seemed to enjoy Jade's singing. She smiled when he made attempts to hum along. It dawned on her that she was turning into the spinster caretaker even though she was married. It wasn't a role she saw for herself and she was worried that she wouldn't be able to change the direction her life had taken.

Jade made a surprising discovery that lifted her spirits. Although Old Lau's business burnt to the ground, he had emergency reserves that he kept hidden from his children. His daughter-in-laws suspected he had hidden savings, and would ask Jade if the old man had said anything. Since Old Lau's speech was impaired from the stroke, the answer was the same every day – 'No'.

Under Jade's care, Old Lau's condition improved and even though he couldn't talk, he was more expressive with his face. 'Are you feeling all right? Either you're having facial spasms or you're gesturing with your face. Are you trying to tell me something?' Jade said to Old Lau. 'Blink once for yes and twice for no.'

Old Lau blinked once.

'Is there something under the bed?'

Old Lau blinked again.

'All right, I'll take a look if you insist.' Jade was curious. She looked under the bed but couldn't see anything. Then she felt around under the bed and found one floorboard that was loose.

'There's a secret compartment!' Jade whispered in excitement. 'What are you hiding here?'

At the onset of the Japanese invasion, Old Lau was clever enough to convert some of his assets to gold, silver and jewelry. Jade couldn't understand why Old Lau chose to tell her about the whereabouts of his safe – perhaps it was to thank her for taking care of him, or maybe he thought that she was his wife. If his children had paid more attention to the old man, they might have found the secret hoard. She couldn't be conspicuous with the money even though she knew where it was hidden.

'Thank you for trusting me,' she said. 'I will keep your secret.'

She felt sad that she finally had the means, but was unable to save Little Pig. It was important she survived the war in order to benefit from the newfound wealth which she had to squirrel away before Old Lau's sons discovered the deception. She counted on this money to get her back on her feet once the war was over.

Jade remained in the Lau household till the end of the war. As gatherings were illegal, the Laus kept to themselves like everyone else did. They didn't trust outsiders, who could be spies. The Laus were especially wary of Mr Tsang because of his Japanese employers and didn't want to be associated with him.

Wing told Jade, 'As long as you are in our household, you will have to obey our rules. You are not allowed to invite him into our house. If you must see him, you have to be discreet. We don't want our neighbours to think we're conspiring with the enemy.'

Mr Tsang was only allowed to come by the house early in the morning before the neighbours were up and his meetings with Jade were always brief. When Mr Tsang didn't visit, Jade wondered if he had other lovers. She knew that men had needs. As with his job, she didn't ask and he didn't tell.

Jade was worried for Mr Tsang when she heard that the Japanese had surrendered in Nanjing. She had not seen or heard from him for weeks. Although there was much celebration on the streets once the war was over, there was also revenge for those who were thought to be collaborators with the enemy. *Hanjians* (traitors to the Chinese) were hauled out and beaten in the streets by the public for their wartime activities.

She was overjoyed when Mr Tsang finally turned up and revealed his true identity.

'I beg your forgiveness. I have not been honest with you. I am a double agent for the Communist Party of China. I have been collecting information about the Japanese under the guise of working for them. I couldn't reveal myself to you for fear of compromising your own safety.'

'I'm glad you're safe! Your mother always praised you for being a good son. I had no doubt that you were honest – not a traitor, as people said.'

'I know you believed in me. Now that the war is over, I don't have to hide anymore. I would ask you to marry me but I have to join my comrades in their fight against the Kuomintang. Will you wait for me?'

'Of course I will,' Jade said coyly. She neglected to tell him that she was still married. To her, the Gold Mountain guest husband did not exist.

Life was far from normal after the Japanese surrendered. The economy ground to a halt during the war and intensified fighting between the Nationalists and the Communists meant recovery was nowhere in sight. No sooner did one war end than another began.

It was not until 1949, when Mao Zedong founded the People's Republic of China, that Jade had a chance to reinvent herself. When Old Lau died, she was told there was no longer any need for her in the Lau household.

In the new China, women were encouraged to step out of the house. She wasted no time getting herself a nursing job by bribing a hospital administrator. By the time Wing's wife had discovered the hidden safe under Old Lau's bed, she had already moved into the assigned housing at her *danwei* (work unit), along with her secret riches.

Wing and Ting made a scene by confronting Jade at the hospital.

'You must have known that our father had hidden away this money and not told us. Give it to us or we'll report you to the authorities!'

'What money? You're making false accusations. I should be the one reporting you to the authorities. If I had money, would I still be working in a hospital? Why would you suspect your father of hiding money from you? You should be ashamed of yourselves.'

Her cousins were stumped. They had no proof that the money ever existed. It was her word against theirs if they went to the authorities. They made a hasty retreat when the hospital security guards turned up to break up the commotion.

As the saying goes, 'Without the wind there are no waves.' Nurses started speculating that Jade had cheated an old man of his lifelong savings. She was furious, but kept her composure. After all if she did not flaunt her wealth, no one could accuse her of having ill-gotten gains.

It was a rude shock when she returned to her apartment to find the door ajar. Inside, the room was in disarray. Someone had ransacked her closet and stolen the suitcase containing the money. All her valuables were gone.

'Where were you when the thief broke into my apartment? If you didn't let any strangers in, it must be one of the residents here. I demand you check everyone's room!' Jade lost her temper with the security guard of the housing compound.

Jade reported the theft to her work unit leader, in order that a search could be conducted. Her neighbours were unhappy that they were suspects. In the end, the suitcase was nowhere to be found. Since she did not declare the stolen items except the suitcase itself, no search was undertaken for the valuables.

It was as though the gods had played a cruel trick on her. She was destined to suffer in life. She couldn't even confront her colleagues because she wasn't supposed to have the money. Her saving grace was Mr Tsang.

The first thing he said when they met again was, 'Will you be my wife?'

'Of course, it would be my honour!' Jade was overjoyed.

'You make me a very happy man.' He squeezed her tight. 'We will have a grand wedding.'

'I don't need a grand wedding to make me happy. I just need

you. As my parents died during the war, we can discard with formality.'

'That make sense, since my mother is no longer with us either. Our comrades are our family now. They will be our witnesses.'

And so it was. Jade and Mr Tsang had a civil ceremony. Jade promptly moved in with her new husband, who was now a deputy director in the municipal planning bureau. She vowed that one day she would punish the neighbours who had robbed her.

When Long told Phoenix that the war was over, she could hardly believe they had been lucky enough to survive.

'The gods finally answered our prayers. Freedom at last! Every time we have had to hide from the Japanese soldiers I feared for our lives.' Phoenix cried with joy as she hugged Jing Jing and Kyong Kyong.

'Once the schools are reopened, I can give up farming and go back to teaching again.'

Teacher Deng, who had been appointed as the village head by the Nationalist Government during the war, called for a celebration. Everyone happily shared what little they had. The festive mood was dampened when one of the neighbours mentioned that the civil war between the Nationalists and Communists had resumed now that they'd chased out the common enemy.

In private, Teacher Deng warned Long that the Kuomintang was losing ground. 'There will be repercussions for us if the Communists take charge. We cannot afford to lose!'

For days, Long mulled over what Teacher Deng said and finally told Phoenix his concerns.

'Phoenix, the Communists are winning and that will be disaster for those of us who support the Kuomintang.'

Phoenix finally lost her patience at his bragging. 'People only know that you're with the guerrillas because you keep talking about your escapades!'

'Listen to me. I'm serious. I'll be in trouble if I stay – anyway I can't earn any money as a farmer or a teacher in this environment. We can provide a better future for our children if I go to Hong Kong.'

'In all honesty I've thought about that myself. We should go together.'

'You think like a woman! We don't know what to expect in Hong Kong. How can I concentrate on getting work if I have to worry about feeding all four of us? It's best that I go on my own and send for you when I've found a job and a place to live. The children need some stability. If you stay in the village, you don't have to worry about food and shelter for the time being.'

'If that's the case, you have to work hard so we can be reunited. The children need their father!'

Long promised to send for her and the children as soon as possible, then cycled to Macau and sailed all night to Hong Kong. His plan was to seek assistance from the Cheng brothers Ming and Kong, since they owed him a favour.

Alone, Phoenix was now the mother and father to her two children. Each morning she fed Jing Jing and Kyong Kyong and left them in the care of their neighbour, so she could work in the rice fields as her husband did. She wasn't raised to be a farmer but she did what she had to do to survive. Her back was sore and her hands were covered with calluses, but she told herself it was all worth it when her children welcomed her home at the end of each day.

Long was not the only one who left the village during the civil war. Teacher Deng gave up his role as village head when he left to work for the government in Nanjing. The village tyrant, Hong Fok, assumed the role on the basis that he was a direct descendant of the village founder Hong Sum, and that the majority of the villagers were Hongs. Hong Fok didn't care for politics. He wanted to get ahead regardless of the government in power.

Hong Fok's father used to sell opium in the village. Even though opium was illegal, no one dared to stand up to him because of his connections to the Triads. The elder Hong was generous with his wealth and was known to be openhanded with old people, widows and orphans. Hong Fok, on the other hand, begrudged his father for sharing their money.

During the Japanese invasion, the supply of raw opium was affected by trade disruptions between China and its neighbouring countries. Hong Fok's father saw an opportunity to sell the stockpile of coal that he would have otherwise used to fire his ovens for cooking opium. That business plan, however, was short-lived.

When the Japanese received a tip-off that Hong Fok's father was selling coal on the black market, he was taken prisoner and starved to death for disobeying the ration quota. Hong Fok could do nothing to save his father. He suspected that Phoenix was the traitor because she was also selling coal illicitly.

'Long's wife is a snake – she's the one to blame for your death. Everyone knows she's getting coal from the guerrillas and selling it on the black market. She has a monopoly on the coal supply now that you're dead ... I'll make sure she gets what she deserves!' Hong Fok swore on his father's grave.

The person who tipped off the Japanese was actually a rival opium dealer. People bought coal from Phoenix because she charged less than Hong Fok's father. Instead of taking advantage of the monopoly, Phoenix stopped selling goods when he died because she was afraid for her own safety.

When Hong Fok became the village head, the first thing he did was to summon Phoenix to a village court hearing. His intent was to charge her for being a counter-revolutionary because she supported guerrillas who were pro-Nationalists. Other village elders were aware of his plans and warned Phoenix, as they were afraid she would not be given a fair trial.

'You're in a precarious position,' Hong Fok's uncle warned her. He was indebted to Elder Cheng and this loyalty led him to speak out. 'If you stay for the trial, you will most likely be convicted as a counter-revolutionary. If you leave without standing trial, you will be a runaway suspect and a warrant might be put out for your arrest. In any case, Hong Fok is out to get you – he thinks you're to blame for his father's death. You're not the only one he's after. Fok wants to confiscate the property from all Kuomintang loyalists like Teacher Deng. He's going to tear the village apart with his ambition!'

'Thanks for warning me ... This is worse than I thought. He would not find any grounds to convict me as a traitor. On the other hand, everyone knows Long and I helped the guerrillas – I don't know anyone in the village who wasn't sympathetic to them. After all, they were fighting the Japanese invaders.' Phoenix sighed. 'I have to think carefully about what to do.'

Phoenix knew it would be dangerous for her to stay. She had to leave the village with the children and seek refuge with her second mother and Choy.

That night, she uncovered the silver coins she had hidden in the kitchen hearth and wrapped them in her waistband. In the morning she told her neighbour that she was taking the children to the farm, instead of leaving them behind like she normally did. It was not a surprise since Jing Jing and Kyong Kyong at ten and nine were old enough to help out.

'Mother, are we going to harvest the rice today?' asked Kyong Kyong.

'We are going to visit your grandmother Mei, but you can't tell anyone. It will be a surprise – she'll be excited to see you both!'

The children were puzzled but happy to go on a trip. It was the first time they had left the village, since it was dangerous to travel during the Japanese occupation and the Chinese civil war.

Phoenix and the children walked to the farm, like it was any normal day. Once they got there, Phoenix piled the children into the ox-drawn cart and headed for her ancestral village. When she left the house she knew there was no looking back. She was now on the run from the law. If she was caught, the consequences were dire.

She knew they had to leave China. The question was how.

As predicted, Grandmother Mei was overjoyed to see Phoenix's children. She still didn't have any grandchildren of her own. Choy's drug addiction had probably affected his fertility, so he didn't have any children with Ah Lan.

'I'm so glad you came! If only your father and mother could see your children now ...'

'Every day I light incense to thank them for watching over the children.'

'We are indeed fortunate to have their blessings. I hope all is well – you look troubled.'

'The new village head is calling for punishment for all pro-Nationalists. Long and I are both associated with guerrillas who fought with the Kuomintang army but Long has escaped to Hong Kong and I am alone to face trial for these alleged crimes!'

'You can stay here for as long as you like. We don't have much to offer, but we won't let the children go hungry.'

'Thank you, Second Mother. I'm making plans to join Long in Hong Kong. He hasn't sent for me yet but with the current situation it's best that we leave China as soon as possible. Have you heard from Jade? At the start of the Japanese invasion Choy said her adopted daughter was kidnapped and needed money. I gave him the dragon phoenix gold bracelet that I received from Father as my dowry.'

Mei looked visibly shocked. 'She didn't tell me about her daughter. Now I understand why she came home. She should have confided in me, Choy didn't tell me anything either. Jade seems to be plagued with bad luck. It is very generous that you helped her. We haven't seen her since – I don't know whether she's dead or alive! Your brother is no better off. He was forced to quit smoking opium because there was no supply during the conflicts. All these years of addiction have done irreparable damage. He now smokes tobacco. He doesn't have the strength to do any strenuous work so he sits at home while his wife Ah Lan tends to the farm. She may be Tanka but we are lucky to have her – she's a hardworking daughter-in-law.'

'I know everyone's scraping to get by. We won't stay long. Do you know if Ah Lan knows people who can take us into Hong Kong?'

'The Tanka are people of the water. Given their experience with the waterways in Canton and Hong Kong, you will certainly be able to get out of China as long as you can pay for your safe passage.'

'I'll talk to her.'

The Communist Party posted guards between Hong Kong and Shenzhen to stop the flood of refugees out of China. There were people like Ah Lan's Uncle Liu, who made a living from escorting people from China to Hong Kong. For the right price he would take them out on his fishing boat in the middle of the night and sail to Tai O, a fishing village on Lantau Island.

Phoenix had only enough money to pay for one adult and one child. She had to make the painful decision who to leave behind. Jing Jing was old enough to help out in the house, but Kyong Kyong was their only son and Long would never forgive her if he came to any harm. She decided to leave Jing Jing with her grandmother – Mei promised to take care of her until Phoenix could send for both of them. Mei would be Jing Jing's guardian on the journey. Phoenix treated Mei like her own mother and was prepared to take care of her in her old age.

While Phoenix made preparations to leave, Ah Lan was tempted to tell her about what Choy had done with her bracelet. She felt terrible remorse, hearing that Phoenix had to leave Jing Jing behind.

'Choy, why don't you ask Fung to return the bracelet? Phoenix needs the money. She can only take Kyong Kyong with her to Hong Kong. Jing Jing will be separated from her father, mother and brother.'

'Are you crazy? Do you think Fung will let us have the bracelet out of the goodness of his heart? He will ask us for money we don't have. You better keep quiet about this. Don't bring it up with Phoenix or mother – or anyone for that matter!'

While she disagreed strongly with his actions, Ah Lan was afraid of the retribution he would suffer for cheating his own family members.

7

Worlds Apart

Leaving his wife and children behind, Long made his arduous trek to Hong Kong. He cycled for days to get to the border on an old rusty bicycle left over from the Japanese invasion. He carried a small bag of cooked rice grains and ate a handful each day to save time and money. His determination drove him to push on, even when his legs were in agony from the continuous exertion.

Long joined the sea of people with Kuomintang ties at Lo Wu, all trying to flee Communist China. It was like the Japanese invasion all over again, except now people wanted to leave China instead of getting in. There were hundreds of people, young and old, jostling each other to cross the narrow footpath along the railway bridge into Hong Kong with their worldly belongings on shoulder poles. Every step they took meant they were one step closer to salvation on the opposite side of the Sham Chun River.

Long was surprised and relieved that he had no trouble getting into the British colony, which had no immigration restrictions at that time. It was almost an anticlimax once he crossed over into Sheung Shui. It was a vast countryside no different from the one he left behind, except here he had no food and shelter.

Long approached an egg merchant who was crossing the bridge, carrying his wares. 'Uncle, I just came over from Xinhui. I need to find work. Can you give me any advice?'

'Young man, you will have a hard time if you have no relatives in Hong Kong to host you. There are so many people coming here each day for food and shelter. If you are willing to do hard labour, you may find work at the Cha Kwo Ling mine. Talk to that man with the truck, he can take you into town for a fee.'

'Thanks Uncle, but I don't have much money. Can't I walk there?'

'Well … you could see if he would take your bicycle as payment instead. We are surrounded by hills here. It may take you days if you try to walk, you may even get lost or injured. You'll be better off going with him.'

Fortunately for Long, the driver was willing to take him in return for his old bicycle. The truck quickly filled up with passengers and made its way into the urban part of Hong Kong. Long soon found that not all of Hong Kong was the paradise he had imagined. Cha Kwo Ling was a shantytown of scrap metal and wooden planks, amidst farmlands and fishponds.

Just like the egg merchant predicted, the foreman at the mine was hiring.

'I don't care if you can read and write. I need arms and legs. If you work hard, you get paid. We have no room for free loaders,' the foreman warned Long.

'I will work hard. I won't disappoint you. Thank you for giving me this opportunity.'

He barely had enough to pay his rent, but it was a start. During the day he cut granite with a heavy hammer. At night he looked longingly at the brightly lit Victoria Harbour from the makeshift hut he now called home. For food, he relied on handouts from welfare organisations and he drank from the public tap. He needed to save enough money for Phoenix and his children to join him.

He thought about what the egg merchant said about support from relatives. Maybe the Cheng brothers could help him? They were the only relatives he knew in Hong Kong. The question was how to find them. He approached Mei Ho, a welfare worker who distributed basic necessities to the residents in the squatter settlement.

'Mei Ho, I have relatives who are also from Xinhui, living in Hong Kong now. Do you know how I can find them if I don't have their addresses?'

'You can try the clan associations and business chambers. If they are merchants, you may want to check with the Chinese Chamber of Commerce, since most merchants from Siyi are members. If you like, I can help you.'

Long was filled with hope and gave Mei Ho his heartfelt thanks. He wrote down the names of Cheng Ming and Cheng Kong on Mei Ho's notepad, along with a plea for help.

Dear Ming and Kong,
I hope you are well. I have recently left Communist China due to my connections with the guerillas. I am now working in a mine in Cha Kwo Ling to support myself. It is hard to make ends meet and save to bring the family to Hong Kong. I will be grateful if you can recommend me for any job that provides better opportunities.
    With warmest regards,
    Cheng Long.

He didn't know if he would be successful locating the Cheng brothers, but he had to try. His work as a miner was risky and not well paid. He needed a stable job and a decent place to live before he could send for his family. Each day that passed, he heard stories about the hardships suffered by families left behind.

At the noodle stand, Long overheard one lady telling another, 'I had to leave with my children. We were harassed daily for being counter-revolutionaries. I still don't know whether my husband made it to Hong Kong – but if I'd stayed, we would have died.'

He found out from fellow miners that the truck driver who dropped him off at the mine would be able to smuggle letters back into China and there were Communist border guards who could be bribed to keep one eye closed. Long paid the truck driver with his hard-earned savings to pass a letter to Phoenix telling her he'd made it to Hong Kong, but needed more time before he could send for her and the children. He didn't know that Phoenix was already in trouble.

Hong Fok was furious when he found out that Phoenix had secretly left the village. He suspected someone close to him had told her about his plans.

'One of you must have warned her!' Hong Fok confronted the other members on the village committee.

'It's not a surprise. She obviously had a guilty conscience and ran away,' said Hong Fok's uncle.

'How dare she get away without facing punishment! She's probably in Hong Kong now with her husband.'

'We can put out a warrant for her arrest so she can't escape judgment,' suggested another village elder.

'Let's do that, since Long's wife is a fugitive and he is a counter-revolutionary! Their house belongs to the state,' Hong Fok declared. With that, he confiscated their house and land.

It was a sly move to enable Hong Fok to gain more control in the village. The Hongs already owned most of the land; the other villagers belonged to different lineages and had less say in community affairs. His plan was to accuse those who supported the guerillas during the Japanese invasion as counter-revolutionaries, so he could put them in jail and seize their properties.

His justification was that since he acted on behalf of the Communist Party, he represented the rule of the land.

Phoenix and Kyong Kyong hid in the bottom of Uncle Liu's fishing junk with five other people to cross the Sham Chun

109

River. Kyong Kyong, at nine years of age, didn't know how to swim. He hadn't been on a boat before and was traumatised as he saw water leaking in through the seams of the hull.

'Mother, will the boat sink? Are we going to drown? How long before we get to land?' Kyong Kyong clung on to his mother.

'Don't worry, little one. Uncle Liu is very experienced. He will take care of us. Just try to keep still,' Phoenix whispered, trying to comfort her son despite her own fears.

Both mother and son were overjoyed to see Victoria Harbour.

'Mother, I can see Hong Kong!' Kyong Kyong shouted excitedly. 'Is Father going to be waiting for us at the harbour?'

'Not yet, but we'll see him soon,' Phoenix lied to her son. She wondered how and when she would find Long.

Phoenix was thankful that Uncle Liu's relative was willing to put up her and her son on their sampan in Causeway Bay, but she knew Kyong Kyong would not do well living on the water. She had to find Mei's relative Aunty Poon, who could help them.

Before they left, Mei had written down Aunty Poon's name and address in Hong Kong, assuring Phoenix that she was a good person and would take care of them.

The first thing Phoenix did when she got ashore was to ask directions to Aunty Poon's home. Fortunately, it was a just a short walk from Causeway Bay Pier where they had landed.

All Phoenix knew about Aunty Poon was that she was a very capable woman who took over the running of a chicken and duck stall in the Central Market after her husband died.

Aunty Poon's flat was on the fifth floor of an eight-storey residential building. It was the tallest building that Phoenix and Kyong Kyong had ever been in. By the time they got to Aunty Poon's flat, they were both sweating and breathless.

'If we keep climbing, we'll reach the sky!' Kyong Kyong told his mother.

Phoenix smiled at her son. 'Be a good boy and greet Grand-aunt Poon when we see her – but don't interrupt when we're talking!'

She knocked on the door.

A little girl around Jing Jing's age appeared at the metal grille gate. 'Who are you looking for?'

'I'm looking for Aunty Poon. I am Phoenix Wong, daughter of Wong Ting Fuk. My second mother is Mei.'

'Grandmother, there is an aunty looking for you!'

Phoenix peeked in the flat through the gate and saw a short, round woman walking towards the door. She patted the little girl on her head. 'You're a good girl, Ka Ling. Now go do your homework.'

Aunty Poon looked at Phoenix and smiled. 'You look like your mother, Ling. Come on in!'

Kyong Kyong remembered his mother's instructions and said, 'How are you, Grand-aunty Poon?'

'What a good boy! Your son?'

'Yes, this is Kyong Kyong. I also have a daughter Jing Jing who is still in China. This is our first day in Hong Kong. My husband Cheng Long came down before we did – but I don't know where he is.'

'It sounds like you need work and a place to stay.'

'Yes, I do. I have to earn money so I can get Jing Jing to Hong Kong.'

'Well, you came at the right time. I need help with my laundry business. My son picks up and drops off laundry from office workers around the neighbourhood. I used to do the washing and ironing myself in the evenings but my back has been hurting me lately – anyway I have to wake up early to run the chicken and duck stall. If you are interested, I will pay you two dollars a day, as well as subsidised food and board here for you and your son.'

'Thank you, Aunty Poon. I will work hard, you won't be disappointed. Kyong Kyong, say thank you to Grand-aunt Poon.'

'No need to be so polite, we're all family! Let me show you to your room. You can share a bunk bed with your son. I'll introduce you to the other tenants when they come home.'

111

Within an hour of arriving in Hong Kong, Phoenix was settled in to her new life.

Jing Jing often slept with her window open so she could look at the stars as she lay in bed. She missed her father, mother and brother. If not for Grandmother Mei, she would be alone.

Every day, she wished for a letter from Hong Kong. She wanted desperately to be with the rest of her family. Although Mei was her grandmother, she had not spent much time with her before now; she was closer to her babysitter neighbour in her own village.

Looking on the bright side, she could go to school here. She enjoyed playing with the other children and learning new things. Even though she didn't go to school during the war, her father had taught her to read and write.

The schoolmaster made her the class monitor as she was more advanced in her studies than the other children, whose parents were mostly illiterate.

The special attention from the teachers alienated her from her classmates. Ever since she became class monitor, she was always the last one to be picked for teams.

'Ah Hua, why are the other children not talking to me?' Jing Jing asked her best friend after school.

Ah Hua stared at her feet and looked uneasy. She liked Jing Jing, but didn't want to be ostracised by the others because of their friendship.

'They say your parents are counter-revolutionary and fugitives wanted by the law. I can't be your friend.'

Jing Jing watched Ah Hua run off to join the others.

When she got home Jing Jing asked her grandmother, 'Why do the children in school say my parents are counter-revolutionary and fugitives?'

'Jing Jing, that's not true! Your parents are honest, hard-working people who love China. They left China to find a better life for you in Hong Kong. Don't take to heart what people say.'

112

Mei tried to console Jing Jing, but was worried about the inevitable question.

'When are they coming back for me?'

'I don't know, Jing Jing. They need to work and earn money so they can provide for you and your brother. Be patient. Don't you like living with me?'

'Yes, Grandmother Mei! I hope you move to Hong Kong too!'

'Let's see about that. I am old and quite comfortable here in the village. Just like your mother misses you, your Uncle Choy will miss me if I leave.'

Jing Jing and her grandmother didn't realise that the playground incident would foreshadow events that would unfold across China.

As the years went by, Jing Jing's hope diminished. She didn't dream about going to Hong Kong anymore. She continued to receive letters but they would arrive opened and inspected – without the money her mother said she had enclosed. It was through these letters that she reunited her mother and her father.

Unfortunately for her, strict border controls made it almost impossible for her to join her family in Hong Kong. The Chinese needed to apply for exit permits to leave the country; these permits were not issued freely. She needed to have a very strong case.

Jing Jing was worried that Grandmother Mei would be alone if she left; Uncle Choy didn't seem to care for his mother. She focused on her studies to get ahead – anything to avoid working on the farm like her Aunty Ah Lan.

'Jing Jing!'

Jing Jing was walking from school wrapped up in her own thoughts, when she heard someone call her name. She turned around and saw Ah Hua hiding in the doorway of someone's house.

'Ah Hua! How are you?' She was surprised that Ah Hua was talking to her.

'I shouldn't be telling you this, but I like you and I don't want you to be hurt.'

'What's going on?' Jing Jing could tell that Ah Hua was serious.

'The Communist Party has set up a peasant association to implement a class system in the village. Since your grandparents and parents are landlords, you've been labelled a bad class element too. The State is going to take over your grandmother's property and land.'

'My grandparents and parents have lost everything of value during the war! All Grandmother has is the roof over her head and a rice field to provide us with food. How are we going to survive if the house and farm are taken away?'

'I don't know, Jing Jing, I'm just here to warn you … I know your parents are in Hong Kong. Can't you join them?'

Jing Jing ran home to tell her grandmother. There was already a group of peasants waving pitchforks angrily, demanding Mei turn over the property and the land she owned to the State. Grandmother Mei was caught by surprise. She had lived alongside her neighbours harmoniously for years. The same people now behaved like she was a criminal.

'This is my home! My husband left it to my son. You can live here too, but don't throw us out!' Mei cried out for sympathy.

Jing Jing rushed forward to protect her grandmother as some of the crowd began to jostle the old lady. 'Stop it! What right do you have to take over the possession of our house?'

A village activist stepped out with a document in his hand. 'According to our land survey, your grandfather was a landlord and now that your grandmother and uncle have inherited his property, they are also landlords. No one is allowed to have private property in new China. Every household will have an equal portion of land that they will cultivate for the State. The State will feed and clothe everyone.'

Jing Jing was crushed. The world around her was crumbling.

Choy was already on the run when the troubles started at home. He had heard about the land reform and bribed the peasant association leader in return for a lower-class status. His plan was to sell off what he owned and convert that to cash. Unfortunately, he underestimated the loyalty of the peasant association leader. Not only was he going to lose his land, but also face a charge of bribery.

He had to leave China or face prison, but had nothing of value to pay for his safe passage. He was desperate when he came up with the idea of selling Jing Jing as a child bride. In the old days, she would have already been betrothed at thirteen.

Uncle Liu's friend Mr Chiang was looking for a daughter-in-law; a bride for his son who was mentally handicapped. It was his only son and he wanted grandsons to carry on the family name. Mr Chiang promised to pay Choy ninety-nine silver dollars and his voyage to Macau in return for the bride.

Choy and Mr Chiang went back to his mother's home in the middle of the night to take Jing Jing away by force.

'We have to discuss how we do this. If we make a mistake, the girl will scream. I don't want to wake up my mother.'

'Judging from your bony frame, I doubt you can do the heavy lifting. The girl probably weighs more than you,' Mr Chiang smirked. Choy ignored his remarks.

'If you can pin her down, I'll gag and bind her. Then you can slip the rice sack over her head.'

'I can't imagine how you treat your enemies if you treat your own niece like a dog for slaughter,' sighed Mr Chiang, shaking his head.

'How I treat her is none of your business. I have a clear conscience. You should question your own morals, you're the one buying her!' Choy retorted. 'Let's get going. The girl is in the back room.'

Jing Jing was fast asleep when the two men started to work together to pin her down and gag her, but she was soon startled awake. In the dark she couldn't see who it was. As soon as she opened her mouth to scream, Choy stuffed a rag into it. He moved quickly to tie her up.

Jing Jing was in pain and continued to shout for help, but her screams were muffled. Soon a rice sack was slipped over her head. She couldn't escape no matter how hard she tried.

Without an exchange of words, the men completed their evil deed. After Mr Chiang carried Jing Jing away on his shoulders back to his boathouse, Choy woke his mother up.

He came straight to the point. 'Mother, please forgive me! I need money to leave China. I have sold Jing Jing as a child bride. I'm leaving tonight for Hong Kong – I've asked Ah Lan to take care of you.'

'Are you out of your mind? How can you do this to your niece?' She frantically got up to look for her granddaughter. 'Jing Jing! Where are you?'

'Mother, she's gone already ... She will be well looked after. Don't worry.' Choy tried to placate his mother, who didn't even seem to care that he was leaving China.

'She's only a girl! Her mother entrusted her to our care – you don't have the right to sell her. It's my fault. I have raised you badly!' Mei wept.

'If I don't escape China, I will be tortured by the Communist Party for bribing the peasant association leader.'

'You should stand up for your own mistakes. Even as your mother, I can't side with you. Jing Jing is innocent and you have ruined her life. Tell me where she is so I can get her back!'

'Mother, you can't do that. You will jeopardise my safety. Would you rather see your only son go to jail and face almost certain death?'

'I want you to live, but Jing Jing shouldn't suffer for your mistakes. Please tell me where she is! Maybe I can talk the groom's family into letting her go.'

'Sorry Mother, I can't tell you. I'm leaving now. Please take care of yourself.' Choy knew his mother would protest about his methods, but he didn't expect her to be so nonchalant about his departure. 'Please wait until tomorrow morning before sending a search party out for Jing Jing. Otherwise I won't have a chance to get away.'

'I'm ashamed that you are my son. I hope our ancestors won't punish you for what you did!'

Choy walked into the darkness, not looking back. He wasn't going to be soft-hearted and ruin his chance of freedom.

Jing Jing kept struggling from the minute she was kidnapped until her captor stopped walking. She knew she was on a boat from the rocking motions of the waves; she heard whispers but didn't recognise the voices.

Her heart was pounding and her mind racing. Where was she? Had she been kidnapped by pirates? What did these people want from her? How was she going to get out of this situation?

Suddenly the person carrying her rolled her onto what felt like a bed. She panicked and kicked as hard as she could, then heard footsteps leaving the room and the door closing. But she was not alone.

'Don't struggle. I'll let you go,' said a man.

Jing Jing felt the ropes loosen around her shoulders. When the rice sack was lifted, she saw the face of a middle-aged man with a childlike appearance.

'You are so pretty! Father said you are my little bride and will live with us from now on,' said the man-boy with an innocent smile, and held her hand.

Jing Jing pulled away from him. 'There must be a mistake,' she said as she undid her gag and proceeded to untie the rope around her ankle. She stood up. 'Someone brought me here against my will. I'm going back home!'

'Little bride, please don't leave me! I waited a long time for my own little bride. Father said he would hurt you if you leave.' He hugged her and cried. There was no way she could break free.

Jing Jing sensed there was something not quite right about

this man. He wouldn't understand the gravity of the situation, even if she tried to reason with him. She had heard of women abducted as wives in rural villages but never thought it would happen to her.

'Help me! Help!' Jing Jing cried at the top of her voice as the man began to smother her with his overpowering embrace.

'Keep quiet, girl! No one will hear you. We're out at sea now,' said a woman from outside the door.

'Help me! I shouldn't be here. Let me go!'

'Your uncle sold you to us. You are our daughter-in-law now. This is your home – you're not going anywhere!'

'No! That can't be true! My uncle wouldn't sell me – he can't sell me!'

'Well, he did and there's nothing you can do about it. Be good to my son and we will treat you well. If you try to escape, I'll make you pay for your disobedience.'

All the while the man, her supposed husband, kept squeezing her and begging her not to leave. 'Don't leave, little bride. Don't leave.'

'Boy, do what your father told you. You need to control your bride so she doesn't leave.'

'Yes, Mother,' replied the man and proceeded to pull off Jing Jing's clothes.

'Stop it! Help! Help! Rape!' Jing Jing screamed and cried as he tried to undress her. 'No, please! Don't do that!'

'Please don't cry. I don't want to hurt you, little bride.'

His mother was still at the door. 'Boy, don't be shy. She's your bride. You can do whatever you want with her.'

'I don't want her to cry.'

Jing Jing took the opportunity to run to the door. 'Please let me go. My grandmother is alone – I need to take care of her. I promise if you let me go I won't tell anyone!'

'Jing Jing, you are now Chong's wife. You belong here … with him.'

Jing Jing was shocked the woman knew her name. So it was

true! Her uncle had sold her. Why would he do that? How could he do that? Did her parents not want her anymore? She was so frightened and confused. What was going to happen next? She wished this was all a nightmare and she could wake up from it immediately.

'Don't cry. I won't hurt you,' Chong tried to comfort Jing Jing.

'Please let me go. Please ...' The more she cried, the more Chong tried to hug her.

'I'll leave you two alone. It's late now. Don't let her run away – your father will be very angry if she does. He paid good money for her!'

Jing Jing spent the rest of the night huddled in a corner where she cried herself to sleep.

Thanks to Uncle Liu, Choy made it to Tai-O, a fishing village in Hong Kong. He hid in the bottom of the fishing boat to escape the border patrol. According to Uncle Liu, there had been dead bodies floating down the river, presumably people who were caught escaping the mainland. But each day, more and more people risked their lives to leave China.

Choy knew the money he had from selling Jing Jing was not going to last him a long time. When his business was doing well, Elder Cheng opened a bank account in Hong Kong to diversify his wealth. Choy counted on getting access to this money. He had his father's stamp, his will, and a letter from the former village head that certified his death.

Choy didn't know how much his father had in the account, but he hoped it was enough to draw from while he looked for a job. He felt he had enough experience working with his father to obtain a job in a trading firm. He was certain that he was destined for big things in Hong Kong. It was a land of opportunity! He had heard of others who escaped to Hong Kong only to find menial work – but it was not going to be the same for him.

Once he made it to Tai-O, Choy hired a boat to take him to Kowloon. He had no intention of staying in the fishing village. He rented a room at a guesthouse where he got cleaned up before going to the bank. In Hong Kong, people were judged by their appearance. He wasn't going into a bank dressed like he was fresh off the boat.

He had kept a suit from his days working in Canton for his uncle. It was one of the few things he didn't pawn. He felt confident that he would get the money when the Indian doorman at the bank pulled the door open for him – and he was right.

His father had left a tidy sum of Hong Kong dollars that now belonged to him. Choy kicked himself for not leaving China sooner. He could have been living like a king! All this while he put up with his mother's criticism for running his father's business to the ground.

'You look very happy. Did you win the lottery?' the friendly manager at the guesthouse asked Choy.

'No, but close ... I inherited some money from my dead father.'

'Congratulations. Does that mean I don't have to chase you for rent?'

'I won't make life difficult for you.'

'Well, you know what they say about sharing sudden luck ... You should give everyone a treat.'

'Since you are the only one here, I guess I won't go broke giving you a treat. I would like to see more of Hong Kong anyway. What do you suggest?'

'My shift ends in an hour. Let's go to the mahjong school[15] next door – there's free food and drinks. I'm not going to take advantage just because you're a nice chap!'

'I haven't played mahjong in a while. I don't know if I'm up to it.'

'If you lose, just treat it like school fees – paying to learn.'

---

[15] A mahjong school is a licensed venue in Hong Kong where people over 18 can play mahjong.

It didn't take much for Ah Hoi to convince Choy to make his first visit to the mahjong school. And it wouldn't be the last.

*　*　*

Unaware of Choy's arrival in Hong Kong, Phoenix received a shocking letter from Mei.

Dear Phoenix,
I regret to deliver a very bad piece of news. I have let you down. I have not been able to protect Jing Jing. Your brother Choy has sold her as a bride and has since escaped to Hong Kong. I would gladly give up a limb in return for Jing Jing, but no one knows where she is.

Jing Jing has been a very obedient girl. She has been looking forward to seeing you again in Hong Kong. As you know, she has written to you several times. I hope she memorised your address so she can write to you if she's safe.

I will let you know as soon as we find her.

Phoenix nearly collapsed when she read the letter. A million and one thoughts ran through her mind. Was Jing Jing safe? Where was she? How could her brother betray her?

She wanted to go back to China to find her daughter, but her son and husband needed her. Also she would be caught if she went back. It was not a solution.

When she showed Long the letter, he was furious.

'If I get my hands on Choy, I'll tear him to pieces! He doesn't deserve to live!'

'What happened, Father?' Kyong Kyong asked.

'We just found out that your sister is missing! Nobody knows where she is,' Phoenix sobbed as she hugged her son.

'Oh no! We have to find Big Sister! Let's go back to China to look for her.'

'No, son, we can't go back to China. We would be caught. It

121

wouldn't do your sister any good if we are imprisoned – or worse, executed.' Phoenix gave Kyong Kyong the harsh truth so he understood there was no chance of returning.

'But what about Big Sister? She is supposed to be here with us!'

Kyong Kyong's words cut into Phoenix's heart. She regretted not bringing Jing Jing. She could have brought them both to Hong Kong but she wanted to have some savings for their new life. She had every intention of bringing Jing Jing to Hong Kong when they could rent an apartment ...

Even though both Phoenix and Long were working, they had menial jobs and could not afford more than a bed at Aunty Poon's. If not for his sponsors, Kyong Kyong would not be able to go to school. In return, he wrote letters to them through the church telling them about his studies.

Some nights, Phoenix laid in bed thinking about the discrepancy in the lives of her two children. Kyong Kyong studied English at school and was getting opportunities in life he never would have had in China. He helped her assemble plastic flowers to earn extra money in the evenings – but he didn't have to work. He was only expected to study and do well in school.

In her heart she knew if Jing Jing had been born a boy, she would not have left her behind.

8

Escape from Love

'I know you don't care about my son but he adores you, so you should be thankful to the gods for giving you a good husband.'

Jing Jing kept quiet when her mother-in-law lectured her about the obligations of a wife. Chong was like a child trapped in a man's body. What would he know about love? He treated her with the same affection he would a pet rabbit.

Jing Jing knew that Chong could not bear to see her cry and used that to her advantage. He hadn't tried to molest her again since their first night together. She looked for opportunities to escape from the boat. Her plan was to create a ruse with a fire and escape when everyone was distracted.

She knew Chong was afraid of fire because he would get her to light the paraffin lamp every night. One night, she tipped the lamp intentionally and struck a match as the fuel poured out.

'Fire! Fire! Fire! Mother ... help!' Chong screamed as the table quickly caught fire. He hid in a corner of the bed.

Jing Jing was surprised at how quickly the fire spread. Smoke quickly filled the room as she felt her way to the door. She waited for an opportunity to slip out as soon as help arrived. The floor was a sea of flames and the acrid smoke hurt her eyes, nostrils and throat. Why was it taking so long for anyone to hear them?

She also started to panic. 'Chong, we have to break the door down!'

Chong appeared not to hear her. All the furniture was on fire. She slammed her own body onto the door in an attempt to break the lock, but it didn't budge.

'Chong, I need your help! We have to push the door together …'

The bed caught fire but Chong remained in his corner, too afraid to move. She regretted coming up with such a rash idea. She didn't take into account that her in-laws could be away from the boat at the time of the fire. She risked not only her life, but also Chong's.

'I have to save Chong,' Jing Jing thought. 'He didn't do anything to harm me. I can't let him die because of my foolish actions.'

Jing Jing rushed onto the bed to pull Chong to safety. The mosquito netting was on fire and singed Jing Jing's skin as she reached out for Chong's arm.

'The bed's on fire! You need to get off otherwise you'll be burnt to death …'

Chong suddenly realised Jing Jing was in the room with him. 'Little bride, there's a fire – I'm going to protect you!'

Instead of getting off the bed, Chong pulled Jing Jing towards him.

'No! No! We need to get out of the room!' Jing Jing pulled back.

As the room continued to burn, Jing Jing felt light-headed and nauseous. 'I don't feel too well …' She coughed and lost consciousness in Chong's arms.

'Wake up, little bride! Please don't die!' Chong cried as he hugged Jing Jing.

When Chong's parents returned from fishing, they saw smoke billowing from the direction of their houseboat and feared the worst.

'Our boat is on fire! We have to rescue our son!' Chong's mother screamed.

They paddled furiously towards the houseboat, which

exploded before they could draw close. Their sampan rocked violently on the resulting waves.

'Chong! My son!' Chong's mother wept.

'Stop crying! He may be in the water. We need to get closer.' Chong's father clung on to the hope that he might have escaped but as they scoured the area, it was soon clear that there were no survivors.

All that was left was smoldering debris floating on the surface.

'My son died such a miserable death – give me my son back! It must be that girl who started the fire. You should never have brought her back.'

They usually docked their houseboat in a shore-side village but they had moved to an isolated spot to avoid raising suspicion about their new daughter-in-law. No one heard the cries for help from Chong and Jing Jing; they didn't stand a chance.

'No! No! I am not a killer!' Uncle Liu screamed out with his arms flailing.

'Wake up! You're having nightmares again,' his wife soothed him as she shook him awake.

'She was here. That girl was here, dripping wet like she just stepped out from the river. She wanted revenge.' He was so scared that he hung on to his wife for comfort.

'This is getting out of hand. We need to burn offerings and hire a monk to chant mantras to appease her soul.'

'You know that such practices are outlawed by the Communist Party. We will be persecuted for following the "old ways of thinking".'

'What do you plan to do then? You're clearly haunted by an angry spirit. You have lost so much weight in the past few weeks from the stress and restless nights!'

'I have to confess to her grandmother … I think that's what she wants. This was a bad deal and I should not have got involved.'

*   *   *

Grandmother Mei collapsed in Ah Lan's arms in grief when she heard that Jing Jing had died in the boat fire.

'Jing Jing, my little granddaughter! I have let you and your mother down. Please forgive me!' she wailed.

'I am so sorry, Madam Wong. I should not have introduced Choy to Mr Chiang.'

'Whatever you say now won't bring her back! I have to blame my son for making the final decision to sell his own niece.'

'Did you hold my granddaughter Jing Jing hostage? She was kidnapped from my house. You should have returned her to me.'

Mr Chiang and his wife denied any wrongdoing when Grandmother Mei confronted them. After all, they had lost their only child. Mrs Chiang suspected Jing Jing of starting the fire but she didn't have any proof. It didn't matter now, anyway.

'Go away, crazy old woman! Can't you see we are in mourning? Your son said he was the girl's guardian – her mother had abandoned her and run off to Hong Kong. We were doing the girl a favour by providing her with a husband.'

'I am going to call the police on you!'

'Go ahead. Do you have any proof that your granddaughter was with us? Even if she was, there are no remains. Maybe she killed our son and then swam away. We should sue her for murder.'

'How can you twist the situation like that?' Grandmother Mei cried.

'Mother, we can't win this fight. Let's leave these people alone – they lost a son too,' Ah Lan interjected. 'We can only pray to Tien Hou, the goddess of seafarers, that she looks after Jing Jing in the afterlife.'

Grandmother Mei was devastated at the loss of her granddaughter. She wouldn't have survived if not for her daughter-in-law. She expected Ah Lan to leave her when Choy ran off to Hong Kong, but she stayed.

'Ah Lan, I don't know what I would do without you. I couldn't ask for a better daughter-in-law. Tanka or not, you are worth more than gold or silver!'

'Mother, you are my family. It's my duty to take care of you.'

'If only Choy felt the same way.' She sighed as her eyes welled with tears at the thought of her miscreant son.

She reflected on how Phoenix and Ah Lan had treated her better than her own son and daughter. She sent a letter to Phoenix at Aunty Poon's, to inform of her Jing Jing's death. It was no surprise when she didn't get a reply, as letters were censored by the Communist Party. She was distraught that Phoenix may not even know that her daughter was dead.

There were rumours of tighter controls in the village. Mei had already lost her property and land – leaving her with one room in her old house. She was now at risk of being taunted as a class enemy by members of the Red Guards at so-called 'struggle sessions', meetings devised to publicly humiliate or punish anyone they thought opposed them.

'Open the door, class enemy Mei, you need to answer for your crime against the people.'

At the door were young boys and girls dressed in uniforms, wearing caps. Mei didn't recognise them as children from the village. They questioned Mei about her husband's business relationships with foreigners, her daughter's connections with the Kuomintang, her son's bribery, and anything that was found to be counter-revolutionary in the eyes of the Red Guards. She was made to kneel on the ground as they questioned her.

'Why do you have this container with foreign words?' one girl shouted as she threw a tin at Mei.

'That is an old biscuit tin that I use to store my embroidery kit. I keep it because it's functional.' Mei flinched as the tin hit her on the head and the contents flew out.

'Liar! You admire what is foreign-made. You collaborate with foreign devils.' The girl, who was young enough to be Mei's granddaughter, rubbed her face on the floor among loose needles and the reels of coloured thread.

Neighbours gathered outside her house but did not dare to interfere. In fact, they cheered as the Red Guards took off their belts and started beating Mei.

'You filthy bourgeois reactionary! Communists should follow a simple and plain life. Your bright colour threads are proof of your materialism. You have to strip yourself of your hedonism.'

Her accuser literally tore off Mei's clothes.

'The old lady deserves some respect,' said a bystander.

'You are a sympathiser if you think she should not be punished,' challenged another Red Guard.

Mei could not fight off her attackers. She whimpered in pain and hung on to her underwear. With her head hung low in humiliation, she sobbed as she stood bared in front of the crowd. How could she face her dead husband, who should be the only one to see her in a state of undress?

'Let me take her place. I will take responsibility for her actions!' Ah Lan pleaded desperately. She was worried her mother-in-law would not survive the ordeal.

The youths ignored Ah Lan and continued beating Mei as though it would have been a sign of disloyalty to Chairman Mao if they stopped. They would have kept on going if Mei hadn't lost consciousness.

'Get up and face the punishment!' shouted one of them.

'Let's not waste time, we'll come back again to interrogate her. There are others we need to educate,' said another.

'Mother, be strong. Don't despair.' Ah Lan swooped in to revive Mei as the Red Guards moved on to their next target.

If not for Ah Lan, Mei would have died from the ordeal. When Mei gained consciousness, she never spoke a word again. Ah Lan thought Mei's voice box was damaged from the beating until she heard her talking in her dreams one night.

'Help! Help! Please – a tiger is coming to get me!' she yelled in a state of panic.

'It's just a dream. Don't be scared, Mother,' Ah Lan whispered as she woke Mei up.

Mei went silent as soon as she was awake. It was as though she was afraid of her own voice. Ah Lan knew then that Mei was in a state of trauma. Ah Lan could not afford medicine to repair her mother-in-law's fragile nerves, so she gave her a mixture of temple ashes and water instead.

The Red Guards never came back again to taunt her but Mei suffered continued humiliation as she was assigned by the village committee to pick pig manure from the streets, wearing a dunce hat that denounced her as a class enemy.

Ah Lan was fortunately spared because she was an uneducated Tanka who married into the Wong family. She worked alongside other peasants in work units on collective farms that once belonged to rich landlords like Mei. She generously shared her food ration with her mother-in-law, even though the food was barely enough for one.

Ah Lan lived in fear of what the Red Guards would do next. She was shocked when she overheard that they were going to attack temples. Regardless of what the Party said about eradicating old customs, Ah Lan felt it was an unforgiveable crime to destroy religious artifacts.

She was determined to save the statue of Guan Gong in the ancestral hall that had watched over many generations of Wongs. They were already having hard times. Who knows what misfortune would befall them if the statue were destroyed?

'Mother, the Red Guards are up to more mischief. They're going to ransack temples and destroy all religious objects. We need to save Guan Gong's statue.'

Mei nodded her head in approval as she held Ah Lan's hand in earnest.

'I will carry the statue up the mountain and hide it in the

ancestral cemetery. I don't think anyone would go to the extent of desecrating the tombs.' Ah Lan was willing to protect their patron god at the risk of punishment from the Red Guards.

That night, Ah Lan crept into the ancestral hall that had been taken over as an office for the Communist Party. Thankfully, no one was around. Ah Lan paid her respects to Guan Gong by kneeling in front of his statue and asking for his forgiveness before taking him off the pedestal. She strapped the statue on her back with a baby sling she had sewed, but never used.

She needed to be quick in order not to be found out. She had to return to her house by dawn, otherwise she would be the prime suspect. In the dark, she crossed numerous paddy fields to reach the burial site of the Wongs. The rain made for a wet and slippery journey up the mountainside. She remembered what the old people said, 'When it rains, Guan Gong is sharpening his blade.' It was a good sign.

Ah Lan was not a brave woman. As she walked into the hillside dotted with graves, she felt her hair stand on end.

'Guan Gong, please protect me from evil spirits and snakes. Please help me get to the resting grounds of our ancestors …' Ah Lan whispered her prayers to the statue.

She had only been up at the family grave a few times with Mei. The area was now overrun with weeds. It had not been cleared since Qingming, the tomb-sweeping festival. Mei was in poor health and could not afford to pay for a caretaker for the burial site. Ah Lan literally stumbled into the tombstone in the dark.

Ah Lan did not have any joss sticks to burn but prayed to the ancestors to forgive her for her intrusion and keep Guan Gong's statue safe from harm. With a hand shovel, she dug into the soft earth next to the communal grave till she had a hole big enough to fit the statue. She wrapped it gently in the baby sling and buried it in the hole. She replaced the dirt carefully so no one could tell that the grave had been disturbed.

With Guan Gong safe from destruction, Ah Lan prayed that he would bless the Wongs and help Mei find her voice again.

*   *   *

Jade, now Mrs Tsang, was lucky to have a strong protector during the Cultural Revolution. Mr Tsang was popular as a municipal deputy director and had no enemies. His contributions during the Japanese war were viewed highly by the Party and no one saw any reason to suspect him of wrongdoing.

Jade knew she was not beyond reproach – her father was a landlord, she was a prostitute and an adulterer. Instead of waiting for things to turn out badly, she took the offensive to instigate attacks on her colleagues at the hospital and thereby eliminate potential threats.

She saw an opportunity to become politically active by joining a political study class, where women discussed the affairs of the state and learnt quotations from Chairman Mao. She spoke freely against discrimination by men in the workplace and quickly gained support from other women.

'Men who abuse their authority in the workplace should not be tolerated. Likewise women who give in to such men are equally to be blamed,' Jade proclaimed at one meeting.

She insinuated that men on the hospital management board promoted women in return for sexual favours. She had no proof that her former neighbours were having affairs with the senior management, but it didn't stop her from making the accusations.

The study group put up posters at the hospital for struggle sessions against the management board, as well as women who had been promoted by men. Jade knew there was underlying dissatisfaction when her former neighbours were promoted and stirred their jealousy into a political rage.

'We should start by looking at who has been promoted without sufficient experience.' Jade was clever not to name names.

'Well, Tao Li and Siu Lan have less experience than any of us

131

but were promoted anyway. I think they should be investigated.'
As Jade expected, one of the other study group members was
ready to point fingers at her two foes.

Tao Li and Siu Lan were both surprised to be hauled up by
their colleagues for exchanging sexual favours for their
promotions. They were bombarded with questions in the middle
of the cafeteria, where the struggle session was held.

'Tao Li, you were seen coming out from a room with Dr Fu
looking dishevelled last Wednesday. Can you explain what you
were both doing?'

'I don't know what you're referring to … I am an honest
person with nothing to hide. As a nurse, my job is to assist the
doctors when required. Sometimes patients get unruly so my
uniform may look untidy after I've helped to subdue them – but
there is nothing inappropriate going on.'

'You say you assist doctors. Do you assist them in their
private needs?'

'No. Please do not malign me. I keep a professional
relationship with the doctors. There is no proof of any indis-
cretion.'

'How would you explain your recent promotion?'

'I have been promoted based on my merits.'

'Are you saying that other nurses don't deserve promotion?'

'I didn't say that. I can speak for my own performance. I
worked hard and continued to improve my nursing skills by
taking classes.'

'Is it not true that you were nominated for these classes by Dr
Fu?'

'That is true. He knew that I was a keen learner and
recognised my potential.'

'I am sure you are keen learner beyond your nursing skills.
You used your charms to seduce the doctor and deprived other
women of a fair promotion!'

'I swear to the skies that I am an honest woman!'

'Shut up! Not only do you have no moral values, you practice old customs of swearing to the supernatural. You are a class enemy! Apologise for your crime!'

Tao Li refused and was slapped into submission. The same thing happened to Siu Lan and both were made to wear a wooden board around the necks that detailed their crimes. They knelt for hours without food or water, while colleagues came by to spit on them and call them names.

Jade felt little remorse when she found out that her colleagues were later sent to labour camps to be re-educated. 'I shouldn't feel bad,' she told herself. 'After all, they were the ones who stole from me.'

Jade thought she was receiving hate mail when she received a letter addressed to Mrs Tsang with no return address. The letter was hand-delivered, possibly to bypass the censorship of the postal service.

Mrs Tsang,
You do not know me but I know you. I have been your husband's lover for many years, even before you two met. For years I have suffered in silence for the one I love. You may have his body but I have his heart. It is I that he dreams of every night, not you. He lies with his heart each time he tells you 'I love you'. He married you as a façade. It is because of you that we are kept apart. I dare you to ask him about his true love and give him the choice to pursue his destiny.

The letter was signed 'Fang'.

Jade was disturbed to be told that Mr Tsang was hiding an affair. He was the only man she had come to trust; he always did the right thing and never wavered in his judgment. To discover that she had been deceived by a man yet again made Jade feel as if her world was tumbling in around her.

She knew that he may have done things that were against his

133

principles when he was a double agent during the Japanese Occupation. She didn't question that he might have taken lovers then. She never asked him and he never volunteered any information about his personal life during the war.

Could this have been one of those lovers? Why should she believe a person whom she had never met? This letter could be a hoax from a jealous admirer. After all, Mr Tsang was an influential person that many women would like to marry, if he was single.

After receiving the letter, she spent many restless nights debating whether to confront her husband. He was a good and loving man. Could she handle the truth if he said he loved someone else? She deserved to know if what his lover said was true.

With that thought she rolled over to her husband and asked, 'Do you love me?'

'Of course I do,' he muttered, half asleep.

'Do you love Fang?'

'Why are you asking me such a question?' His tone of voice changed instantly. He sat up in bed and turned on the light.

'I received a letter from Fang, saying you are lovers,' Jade stuttered. She felt like she was the one being interrogated.

'You are not meant to know about Fang,' Mr Tsang sighed.

'Why are you with me if you are in love with Fang?' Jade sobbed at the realisation that it was true.

'Fang and I are not destined to be together. We have known each other for many years. I have tried breaking up many times – the finality was too hard to bear. It doesn't change the feelings I have for you.'

'Liar! How can you love me if you love someone else? You have been cheating on me with your heart and mind. Why did you get married to me in the first place?'

'When I met you at the orphanage, I was at a turning point in my relationship with Fang. I needed a wife who could stand by my side. You are that woman.'

'Is that supposed to make me feel better? You have let me down. I don't know how Fang can forgive you, because I can't.'

'Fang knows we have no future together.'

'If you can't have a future together, why did you even start the relationship?'

'Fang is a man.'

'What? This can't be happening to me! How can you love another man? You're a monster. Are you sick in your mind? You must be the reason why we're childless!'

Jade flew at Mr Tsang in a violent rage. She tore at his clothes as if to find the real man in him. Here was a man she trusted and yet again she had been deceived. She refused to believe it was her own fault for falling into bad relationships.

'I hate you! You're not a man – you're a low life. How dare you deceive me?'

Mr Tsang did not retaliate, even when she spat at him. He silently put up with her physical and verbal abuse. His non-reaction made her even angrier.

'Are you going to defend yourself? You want everyone to think highly of you but you're nothing but a fake. You are human waste. I am cursed for eight generations to marry someone like you. It is a good thing your mother is dead ... she would be ashamed to have you as a son!'

'Don't bring my mother into this.' She finally elicited a response from Mr Tsang, who grabbed her hands to stop the assault.

She was surprised at the force he used. 'You're hurting me!' she yelped.

'You are a filthy-mouthed bitch! I'm going to show you what a real man is ...' He pinned her down and forced himself on her on all fours.

'Stupid whore ... filthy bitch ...' He kept calling her names as he used her like a cheap prostitute. He had his hand over her mouth to stop her from yelling.

No matter how hard she struggled, she could not break free.

135

She was seething with hatred at being violated by men over and over again.

She refused to show weakness by crying. She disassociated herself from what was happening. She told herself she didn't care. When Mr Tsang sensed that she had stopped struggling, his manhood went limp.

'Ha ha! So that's what you call a real man. Is that the best you can do?'

Mr Tsang retaliated by slapping her so hard that he cut her lips.

'I'm not afraid of you!' Jade continued to taunt Mr Tsang.

'You better shut your smart mouth. I'll make you regret it!'

'If I were you, I would sleep with one eye open. You would be better off killing me now.'

'What do you think you would gain by going against me?'

Jade knew what Mr Tsang said was true. He had friends in high places. He could turn the tables on her and accuse her of being insane; she didn't want to be sent to a mental institution.

'I will break your legs if you dare walk out on me.'

She picked herself off the floor, washed up and went to bed without saying a word. She wanted to bide her time. She had an edge over him. If she had the right opportunity, she would take her revenge.

She decided that as long as they were together, Mr Tsang would have to live in fear of when she might get even.

They both slept on the bed that night, like any other night before that, as if nothing happened.

'I can keep up with this farce as long as I have to,' Jade told herself.

When colleagues asked about the bruises on her face the next day, she told them she tripped in the night and had bitten her lips.

Mr Tsang was no fool. He knew his relationship with Fang could cause him more than his job. He had no choice but to send a cryptic letter to break up with his lover. He knew it would hurt

Fang as much as it hurt him; Fang was his first love – but he had taken other lovers, both men and women. Fang, on the other hand, was faithful to him from the start. Mr Tsang was afraid of the intensity of Fang's love.

It was a blow when the letter was returned stamped, 'Undeliverable – Addressee DECEASED' on the envelope. How could this be true? The Fang he knew loved life ferociously. He was passionate about the warmth of the sun and the smell of rain. Mr Tsang was devastated, angry and guilt-ridden all at once. He pounded his fist in the brick wall so hard that Jade came running out of the house, but the physical pain could not numb the mental anguish.

Jade found him slumped over with his head buried in his bruised hands and saw the letter on the ground. She didn't want to comfort him. She was angry that he was making such a public display over his emotions.

'They are watching and listening all the time. You better pull yourself together if you don't want to join your lover in hell!'

Mr Tsang knew it was true. Life had to go on. He had to live with the fact that he chose Jade over Fang.

Jade's relationship with Mr Tsang became tense. She refused to speak to him and regarded him as the enemy.

When she participated in struggle sessions, she imagined the accused was Mr Tsang. It provided an outlet for her pent-up fury. She accumulated merit points for each time she spoke up against the people being purged.

At home, she spat in the meals she prepared for her husband. He suspected that she may tamper with his food, so he always made her try some first.

Despite what had happened, he expected the same pampering treatment he was used to. Jade loathed the idea of preparing his foot-bath every day. One day she punished Mr Tsang by filling the bath with boiling hot water. He yelped in pain and never asked for a foot-bath again.

137

From the outside they looked like a loving couple; on the inside it was a twisted, tormented relationship. She didn't have to wait long to take her revenge on Mr Tsang. She received a visit from his colleagues, who informed her that he had suffered a stroke at work.

'Comrade Tsang, I'm afraid your husband is very ill. Even if he pulls through the first night, he will probably have paralysis and require full-time care. We will train you to look after him, after he is discharged from the hospital.'

'Thank you, Doctor. I will take good care of him.'

9

Black and White

Choy felt lucky. Not only did he make it to Hong Kong but he also inherited his father's money. He was sure he would win at the mahjong school – and he did.

Ah Hoi congratulated him on his winning hand. 'Luck is on your side. I hope it rubs off on me, too.'

Choy smiled and caught the eye of a woman at the next table. She reminded him of Xi Shi, the flower girl he lost his virginity to in Canton. Beneath the heavy make-up, she looked like she was pretty once but had aged prematurely, with lines under her eyes.

She smiled at him and said to Ah Hoi, 'You're not going to win by standing around. Why don't you try your luck playing the rest of my hand? I'm late for work.'

'Pearl, you can't leave now. You will affect our chi,' complained one of her fellow players.

'Relax, Uncle Lok. You're already winning. Surely you can't be afraid that your luck will run away with me,' Pearl teased him. 'I really have to go now. Thanks, Ah Hoi!'

Uncle Lok continued grumbling after Pearl left. 'I don't know how I put up with her. If she wasn't my late brother's daughter, I would bar her from my mahjong school.'

Choy was very intrigued by Pearl, but kept his questions to himself and concentrated on the game at hand. He was playing to win.

Later that night, Ah Hoi toasted Choy. 'Congratulations! The fortune god is smiling on you!'

'I have to thank you instead! Do you know that woman who was at the mahjong school?'

'Pearl? She's a head-turner, isn't she? I've known her for years. She's Uncle Lok's niece.'

'I bet she has a lot of suitors.'

'Well, she's rejected my advances but I told her if she's still single at forty, I would be willing to marry her!'

'She looked all dressed up. What does she do for a living?'

'She's a hostess at Star River. She's a good girl though, she doesn't sleep with customers like some of the others. Her parents died young, so she's the breadwinner for her siblings. Speaking of the devil, here she comes … Pretty Pearl!'

'Brother Hoi! How did you fare?'

'I lost to your uncle but still made some money. Here are your winnings.'

'Thank you! I have to buy you supper then. Who is your friend?'

'This is Choy. Choy, this is Pearl. Choy is buying me drinks to celebrate his win.'

'That's generous of you. Hope you don't mind me joining in.'

'It is our fortune that you would grace us with your company. The more the merrier. I would be lonely if not for my newfound friends!'

'Choy is new to Hong Kong. He's just inherited his father's fortunes.'

'I would hardly call it a fortune – it's just a small sum to tide me over till I find a good investment.'

'You won't be disappointed. Hong Kong is the land of opportunities.'

'If Pearl was not a hostess,' Choy thought, 'she would be perfect for me!' She was a graceful swan compared to Ah Lan, who was a water buffalo. He wasn't going to tell anyone about his wife at home.

Choy, Ah Hoi and Pearl quickly became firm friends. They often met at the mahjong school and made arrangements to get together after Pearl left work. In her occupation, she was expected to entertain clients at the nightclub and sometimes accompany them for supper outside.

On her free days, she brought her 'sisters' along for supper. Pearl didn't seem to mind that Ah Hoi and Choy flirted freely with all of them. Choy always footed the bill.

Pearl talked about her customers – not to brag, but to disassociate from them. They had excesses that Ah Hoi and Choy weren't used to. These men wore gold Rolexes, drove fancy cars and drank expensive XO brandy.

She wanted to find a husband who could take care of her and her family but she knew her customers just wanted to have fun. She would only be a mistress, not a wife and was well aware that men with status looked for a woman of equal social standing. She did not bear such hopes and wasn't willing to have her feelings toyed with.

'Pearl, why did you turn down Boss Lam tonight?'

'Rose, you know he's married with children. He has only one thing on his mind. I'm not going to give it to him.'

'You set your sights too high. You should be satisfied that a man like him treats you well.'

'I want a man who will value me above everything and not toss me away when someone new comes along.'

Choy thought Pearl winked at him when she said that.

'Good luck finding such a man!' laughed Rose. 'I'm going to set my sights on what's immediately in front of me. I take what I can get.'

'I am in front of you. Does that mean you will be my girlfriend?' Ah Hoi teased Rose.

'Yes … If you can afford me.' Rose batted her eyes and acted coy with Ah Hoi.

'I suddenly feel like a spare part,' said Pearl to Choy. 'Will you walk me home?'

'Certainly!' Choy jumped at the opportunity.

'Even though we've met several times, I feel like I don't know much about you.'

'Maybe we should spend more time together.' Choy reached out to hold Pearl's hand and smiled when she didn't shy away.

Choy reminded Pearl that he had inherited money from his father.

'Since you know many rich people, you may have some suggestions on what kind of business to invest in. I want to make big money.'

'It's true that some of my clients talk about business when they're together but more often than not, they're just looking for a good time. That said, I do know of a businessman – Mr Cheong – who is looking for a partner to manufacture toys for overseas customers.'

'I'm not an expert in that area, I played with crickets when I was growing up. I suppose people can afford to buy toys for their children now that the war is over. Could you set up a meeting with him so I can find out more?'

'Mr Cheong is very easy to talk to. I will sound him out.'

True to her word, Pearl set up a meeting for Choy and Mr Cheong at the nightclub.

It was the first time Choy had visited a nightclub and the first time he saw Pearl at work. She was like a butterfly flitting among a bed of flowers. There were many other hostesses who were beautiful, but Pearl stood out with her genuine smile. He felt lucky to be in her company.

Choy thought it was a waste that she was a hostess. She was good enough to be a mistress, but not good enough to be a wife.

Even though he was not Pearl's boyfriend, he couldn't help feeling jealous when he saw Mr Cheong's hands all over her. He was old enough to be her father. He tried to distract him by initiating the conversation.

'So Mr Cheong, Pearl mentioned that you are in the plastic business.'

'Yes, I have a small factory making toothbrush handles. I'm making good money but there are even more opportunities in toys. I already have connections with foreign toy companies who want to outsource their manufacturing to Hong Kong. A lucrative business, but I need capital to buy new machines.'

'Well, I'm looking for a business to invest in. Maybe we can work something out together?'

Choy made the decision to invest in Mr Cheong's business after visiting his factory. It was a small operation, but Mr Cheong explained he didn't need many people to operate plastic mold machines and assemble the toothbrushes. Mr Cheong even showed Choy the sales orders he had from overseas customers. It was certainly profitable – and was about to get even more so.

Mr Cheong seemed like an ideal business partner. Choy trusted what he saw. He handed over a cheque and expected his money to come pouring in.

Unfortunately, it was all a façade. Mr Cheong was just a bookkeeper at the factory. Through his connections, he arranged for a visit when the manager wasn't in. He was looking for hard cash to pay off a gambling debt.

Choy sensed something was wrong when he returned to the factory and couldn't find Mr Cheong.

'We no longer have a Mr Cheong here. I am the manager, Mr Lam. Is there anything I can do for you?' The man he spoke to was puzzled.

'There must be a misunderstanding. I am Mr Wong, Mr Cheong's partner. I am part owner of this factory.'

'Did you walk into the wrong place? Our owner is my uncle, Mr Yip. What's the address of the factory you're looking for? Maybe I can help you.'

'You can ask the workers, I was here last week with Mr Cheong.' Choy was perplexed.

'Ah Song, have you met this man before? He said he was here last week. Do you know anything about this?' Mr Lam asked his foreman.

'He was with the bookkeeper. I didn't think anything of it because Mr Cheong said this man's relative was interested in opening a factory, so he came by to show him how ours operates.'

'Ah Song, you should know better than to let strangers walk in like that. We fired Mr Cheong a month ago for trying to embezzle money. We would have sued him but gave him a chance since he pleaded that he had to take care of his sickly wife and three children. He obviously hasn't learnt from his mistake!'

'Sorry, boss, I didn't know Mr Cheong had been fired. I'll sort him out if he turns up again.'

'Mr Wong, I'm sorry that you've been misled but Mr Cheong doesn't work here, let alone own this factory.'

Choy was crestfallen and furious. Why had he been so stupid as to trusting a stranger?

'Do you know where I can find this conman? I want my money back.'

'Let me give you his address. Hopefully, he's still there. He may have moved knowing that you'll find out the truth sooner or later.'

Choy immediately filed a report with the police when he didn't find Mr Cheong at the address that Mr Lam gave him.

'Ah Sir, the man is a liar and a thief – you have to arrest him!' Choy made his views clear to the policeman taking his statement.

'He may have lied but you gave him your money willingly. You should have checked his credentials. Don't worry, you're not the first to fall for such a ploy and you won't be the last.'

'Are you saying that it's my fault? I'm the victim and he's the criminal. You should stand for the law and defend my rights!'

'Who do you think you are, raising your voice to me? If you want my help, you better show more respect.'

Choy was indignant but held his tongue. He felt he was getting secondary treatment because he was from mainland China.

All the police told him was to stay home and wait. They didn't share any definitive plan to arrest Mr Cheong.

His friend Ah Hoi urged him to take the law into his own hands.

'My cousin Kwei is very well connected, he can track down anyone in Hong Kong through his network. He means business, he could intimidate Cheong to give you the money back.'

'I don't want to get the secret society[16] involved.'

'Don't worry, Choy. Kwei is my family; you're my best friend. He will treat you like family too. He is very loyal to us. You just need to give Cheong a good scare so he coughs up the money. It's not like we're committing arson – or murder.'

'I wish I hadn't introduced that scoundrel to you. I think Ah Hoi has a good point, at least you can track him down then tip off the police where to find him,' Pearl chimed in.

'All right, let's talk to your cousin.'

No one predicted how this small money matter between two individuals would blow up. Cheong owed a gambling debt to the Righteous Society that he had paid off with Choy's money. Ah Hoi's cousin Kwei, who helped Choy track down Cheong, was from the Red Sun Society.

Kwei gave Cheong a severe beating and threatened to kill him if he didn't return the money to Choy. Cheong was so scared, he sought help from the Righteous Society.

'Crazy Dog Lam[17], you have to help me! I'm in trouble for paying off my debt like I said I would. The money was from a

---

[16] Chinese Triads were known as 'secret societies'.
[17] Triad members tend to go by their nicknames.

business partner and now he's after my life. He's sent a gangster to beat me up and will kill me if I don't return the money!'

'It's your own fault for getting into trouble in the first place. But who's this busybody interfering in our business?'

'His name is Kwei. I'm told he's from the Red Sun Society.'

'These ruffians from the Red Sun Society are going too far to think they can come into our territory and mess with our people. I have to teach him a lesson. They need to know the Righteous Society runs the show here!'

Crazy Dog Lam and his men hunted down Kwei at his usual haunt, a drink stand that Ah Hoi and Choy also frequented.

'How's your cousin Kwei? Is he out of hospital?' asked Ah Sum, the drink stand owner.

'I have no idea what you're talking about. Why would he be in hospital?' Ah Hoi was shocked.

'Don't you know he was beaten up by some guys from the Red Sun Society in the alleyway? He'd just left after his morning tea. I heard that your cousin threatened one of their men Cheong on their territory, so they were retaliating.'

'I had no idea! I'll go straight to my uncle and find out how he's doing.'

'I'll go with you,' said Choy, who looked very nervous.

On their way, Choy asked Ah Hoi, 'Do you think the gang members would come after me next as I was the one who asked Kwei to track down Cheong?'

'I don't know. It seems the matter has escalated to into gang warfare … I'm worried too. Maybe you should keep a low profile for now.'

What Ah Sum didn't mention was that in the process of defending himself, Kwei blinded a young man, the nephew of the Triad leader. Ah Hoi only found this out when he visited Kwei at the hospital.

'We have to make concessions otherwise this will turn very ugly between the two Triads. Our boss doesn't want any trouble from the police. He proposed to make peace.'

Before Ah Hoi could breathe a sigh of relief, Kwei said, 'He will push the blame on your friend Choy, since he is not a member of our Triad.'

'Choy will be slaughtered if you do that!' Ah Hoi was in disbelief. He felt guilty for suggesting the idea to Choy in the first place.

'I'm sorry to give you the bad news. I have no choice, it's either him or me. The men from the Righteous Society nearly killed me. Do you want my sworn brothers to finish the job?'

'This is a huge misunderstanding. Choy just wants Cheong to return his money. He doesn't have a personal vendetta against the Righteous Society. Can your gang leader negotiate on behalf of Choy?'

'I can ask, but no guarantees. What can your friend offer in return for protection?'

'He may still have some money. If I were him, I'd be willing to do anything that your boss asks.'

Ah Hoi regretted having made that last statement.

The Righteous Society Triad leader was willing to forgive Choy if he could come up with compensation for his nephew. Choy gave as much as he could and borrowed the rest from the Red Sun Society. He agreed to work off his loan as a runner, harassing and intimidating debtors who owed money to the Triad.

'I would have been better off staying in China. I'm nowhere close to paying off my debt and yet each day I have to chase debts from other unfortunate souls. I have nightmares about the frightened children who beg me to stop beating their fathers!'

'If you stayed in China, we wouldn't have met!' Pearl tried to comfort Choy. 'I wish I could make things better. I know you can't afford to rent your own room now, so why don't you move in with me?'

Choy was taken aback by her direct offer. He'd been kicked out from the hotel when he didn't pay his rent and was sleeping in the back room of a mahjong parlour operated by the Red Sun Society.

'I'm not suggesting that we sleep together – I'm still looking for my Prince Charming! My siblings and I own the apartment that we live in. I can waive the rent if you can do some handyman work around the house.'

'What a relief! I don't know what would be worse – to be a gangster or a kept man – or both …'

'Kyong Kyong, time to get up. You'll be late for school if you don't hurry.'

'Don't worry Mother. I'm dressed already. I slept in my uniform to save time.'

'Silly boy! Your shirt and shorts are creased! I'm sure to get a note from your teacher. Unfortunately, we can only afford one set of uniform so you'll have to go to school as you are.' Phoenix was perplexed but amused by her son's behaviour.

It was hard getting Kyong Kyong out of bed every day. She felt bad for keeping him up late whenever she needed an extra pair of hands to assemble plastic flowers for extra income. She constantly reminded him that studies came first.

'Be a good boy at school.'

'I know … pay attention in class. Come home right away after school and do your homework. Bye bye, Mother.' Kyong Kyong was so used to the drill, he finished his mother's sentence as he ran out of the house.

Even though he was cheeky, Phoenix knew he was well behaved compared to most boys. He had matured a lot since he left China. In Hong Kong, he had a chance to grow out of his sister's shadow and was no longer the baby.

It was Christmas when Kyong Kyong was called to the staff room in school.

When he first arrived in Hong Kong, he didn't know what Christmas was. He soon learnt that it was a festival widely celebrated by the expatriates. At school, Father John said that Baby Jesus was born on Christmas day to save men from their sins. At home, he stuck green plastic pine needles to artificial branches for Christmas trees destined for American and British homes.

'Kyong Kyong, your sponsors sent you a Christmas card.' Teacher Pang smiled as she handed him the envelope.

'Thank you, Miss Pang.' No one ever wrote to him, let alone someone from overseas. He stared at the young queen on the stamps. His first thought was that he could start a stamp collection.

'Aren't you going to open it?'

Kyong Kyong was eager to read the card but he wanted to savour the moment alone. It was his first letter, after all. Since Miss Pang was very interested, he had no choice but to open the envelope in front of her.

The colour of the red envelope was similar to the red packets he received for New Year. He wondered if Westerners also believed that red was a lucky colour. He carefully opened the envelope so as not to damage the stamps. Inside the envelope was a card with a happy scene of children playing together in the snow.

'So that's what Western children do for Christmas,' Kyong Kyong remarked out loud.

'Why, they'll catch their deaths in the cold like that! It's surprising how Westerners are so relaxed about letting their children play in the snow.' Miss Pang unconsciously drew her shawl over her shoulders as though to ward off the cold.

Something dropped on the floor as Kyong Kyong opened the card. It was money.

'Your sponsors are very generous. Not only did they pay your school fees, they also gave you a Christmas present,' Miss Pang said as she picked up a one-pound note. 'What else is in the card?'

'It reads, "Thank you for keeping us informed on your progress. Keep up the good work. God bless you and your loved ones. Merry Christmas!" It's signed by Thomas and Louise Brown.'

149

'Well, it was good of them to send a card. By the way, one pound is worth sixteen Hong Kong dollars. You better give it to your parents for safe keeping.'

'I will, Miss Pang.'

'Now run along. I'll see you tomorrow,' Miss Pang said as the school bell rang.

Kyong Kyong felt important with the card in his hand as he left the staff room. He debated whether to tell his mother about the money. He was often teased in school about being a poor student who had no pocket money, but now he could impress his classmates by buying comic books and toys with the sixteen dollars.

'Mother, I received a Christmas card from the Browns today. They also gave me one pound. I would like you to keep it for Big Sister. Although I don't have comic books and toys, I'm lucky because I have you. I would be selfish to keep good things to myself.'

'Kyong Kyong, you are a very thoughtful boy. I don't know if your sister would ever …' Phoenix choked on her words. Phoenix had never received the letter Mei sent to break the news of Jing Jing's death. She was living each day with the torment of knowing Jing Jing had been sold by Choy and had vanished from her life.

Phoenix used to tell Kyong Kyong stories about Jing Jing playing with him. She didn't want him to forget his sister. She always ended the stories by telling him that they would soon be reunited and she would take care of him like the wonderful big sister she was.

Since Jing Jing had been kidnapped, Phoenix spoke less and less of her. It was as though she wanted to bury the pain of losing her first born. She couldn't do anything to find her daughter and felt immense guilt for letting her down. When Kyong Kyong spoke of her, it was like all the floodgates opened and her emotions poured out.

'Mother, please don't cry! I don't mean to make you sad.'

'Kyong Kyong, I'm OK. I just miss your sister.' She hugged Kyong Kyong. 'I wish I could bring her home.'

That night, Phoenix dreamt of Jing Jing. She was being pushed along in a sea of people. She heard Jing Jing calling for her.

Each time she reached out for Jing Jing, the person she touched would turn out to be a stranger.

Then she heard loud knocking at the door ... it was Jing Jing's voice again.

'Mother, please let me in!' Jing Jing cried.

'I can't ... The door is locked! I don't have the keys.' Phoenix was frantic. She couldn't get to her daughter.

'Mother, don't leave me out here by myself!'

'Jing Jing, you're not alone. I'm with you, I'm always with you no matter how far or near you are. My blood runs in you and I can feel your pain. Don't despair my dearest child, I will do my best to find you.'

'You're too late. My blood is cold.' The knocking stopped.

Phoenix woke up to find her pillow soaked in her own tears. Long, oblivious to her emotional turmoil, was snoring away. She didn't normally recall her dreams but that one was so vivid, she wondered if it was a message from Jing Jing.

She was in a daze all morning. She confided in Aunty Poon about her dream.

'The neighbours came home late last night. You probably slept poorly because of the noise. With Jing Jing on your mind, it's only natural that you dream about her.'

'It seemed so real, like she was here.'

'It may help if you talk to Mrs Ng across the road. She is a *mun mai poh* who gives very accurate readings.'

Phoenix felt nervous when she approached Mrs Ng at her shop front.

'How are you, Phoenix? Have you eaten? Are you here to buy my sauces to spice up your dinner?'

'Actually I'm here to seek your advice on a personal matter, if you don't mind.'

'Of course I don't mind. I'll ask my daughter to mind the shop while we go upstairs for some privacy.'

Mrs Ng offered Phoenix a cup of tea while they talked.

'I've been having nightmares. I think something bad's going to happen. I am seeking my father's spirit for help and protection.'

'Do you have rice, for your ancestor to identify you?'

'Yes, I do.'

After Phoenix gave Mrs Ng the rice, the medium went into a trance. Her eyes shut and her hands trembled on the table as she travelled into the spirit world.

'There's a woman who wants to speak to you.'

Mrs Ng's voice changed. 'You're a wonderful daughter. You're truly a blessing.'

'Mother!' gasped Phoenix.

'I have let you down. I will make amends in my next life.'

'I don't understand, Mother. What are you talking about?'

'She has left us.' With that, Mrs Ng woke up from her trance.

'Is that it?' Phoenix could not help expressing her disappointment.

'I'm sorry you were not able to speak to your father. I can't control whether the spirits come and go. It seems your mother had a message for you, though.'

'I don't understand what she was saying about letting me down. We lost touch many years ago.'

'I'm happy to give you a free reading another day.'

'Don't look so glum, Phoenix,' said Aunty Poon when she heard about Phoenix's encounter. 'Let's go to the temple tomorrow and make offerings to Guan Yin. She will help reunite you with your daughter.'

Phoenix managed a smile. She knew Aunty Poon was trying hard to cheer her up. She was almost like a mother to Phoenix.

At the temple, Phoenix prayed aloud for Jing Jing's safety.

'Excuse me, I was kneeling next to you and heard you mention my village in your prayers.' A fellow devotee approached Phoenix at the incense urn. 'I just arrived in Hong Kong a week ago.'

'What a small world! So do you know my daughter Jing Jing and my second mother Mei?' Phoenix was ecstatic that someone may have news of her daughter.

'I'm afraid I'm the bearer of bad news ... Your daughter Jing Jing died in a fire and Grandmother Mei, who barely survived the loss, became dumb during a struggle session.'

Phoenix collapsed into Aunty Poon's arms when she heard the news.

'How can heaven be so cruel? Jing Jing never did anything to hurt anyone ... I'll never see her again.'

10

Life After Death

Jade hoped for the worst when Mr Tsang suffered a stroke. Unfortunately he survived, so Jade found herself burdened with the care and feeding of a man she hated with a vengeance. He represented everything bad that had happened to her.

She tried her best to keep Mr Tsang at the hospital. Once he was discharged he was her responsibility. Mr Tsang's work unit paid her to stay at home as a caregiver.

She found no reason to make life more comfortable for Mr Tsang just because he was disabled. She was far from being sympathetic. Mr Tsang was bedridden when he recovered from the stroke. He was totally dependent on Jade for his everyday needs. His speech was impaired, so he couldn't complain when she wasn't taking care of him.

Jade left him in his soiled clothes for as long as she could stand the stench but she made sure her husband and the house were presentable when they were expecting guests.

It could have been out of despair that Mr Tsang did not survive very long after his stroke. She cried at his wake – not from sadness at his passing but from the emptiness she felt. It frustrated her that she couldn't find happiness.

After his death, she couldn't bear to be around Mr Tsang's colleagues. She requested her work unit to allow her to travel back to her hometown. She wanted a change.

*   *   *

Jade wasn't surprised that her mother had passed away and that Ah Lan was the only family member left in the village. When Ah Lan asked where she had been, Jade told her to be glad that she was back. She imposed her authority over Ah Lan, who didn't complain out of respect for her late mother-in-law.

She told the local authorities that she had divorced her American capitalist husband and returned to China to dedicate her life to Mao. No one challenged her story. Instead, she was held up as a role model and asked to share her loyalty and love for Mao at public debates.

She was a consummate actress. She denounced her late father who was a capitalist and swayed the audience with her knowledge of Mao doctrines that she had gained from political study classes. When she wasn't working in the communal kitchen, she decorated the village walls with Maoist slogans. It gave her a new purpose in life.

Jade worried constantly that people would find out about her past. She made Ah Lan collaborate with her story.

'You better not tell anyone that I had amnesia and was working in Guangzhou.'

'That should be nothing to be ashamed of. You had an accident and lost your memory!'

'Just don't talk about it, OK?'

Ah Lan was happy to comply. After all, Jade was the closest relative she had left. It remained that way until China relaxed its closed door policy and Choy came back from Hong Kong.

Choy struggled to make ends meet in the years after he left China, working as a runner for one of the Hong Kong Triads. He was the scapegoat whenever anyone in the Triad got into trouble with the law. Even though he was paid to take the rap and serve the prison term, having a felony record meant no one would hire him for any proper work.

Since he was not officially a Triad member, they offered him little protection in prison. Pearl was a faithful friend to him in the beginning but got tired of visiting prison all the time. When a regular client offered her a high-paying job to run an upmarket bar in Kuala Lumpur, she took it.

On her last visit, she told Choy, 'Much as I like you, I think our lives are heading in different directions. You have been very sweet to me and deserve a lucky break in life but I cannot be waiting for you forever!'

Instead of persuading her to stay, Choy swore at her – calling her a slut – and turned his back on her without saying goodbye. She was the only good thing he could count on outside of prison. It was miserable to think of life without any hope.

When he had finished his sentence, he lived with other poor bachelors in a caged home. His health deteriorated from years of smoking. He finally decided that he had to give up his dream about making it big in Hong Kong and return to China.

Even though Jade had a passion for Mao that could have lasted a lifetime, she was not fortunate in her new lover. Mao died in 1976. He was her husband, her father, her brother, her teacher – her god. She mourned for Mao and continued to wear her collection of Mao pins, even when it became unfashionable to do so.

With Mao's passing came changes. It was a new China that emerged. Some neighbours were critical of Jade's behaviour.

'She behaves like she is a mistress of the house. We are all equals. There is no reason why she should be bossing you around,' one told Ah Lan.

'I agree she has an outspoken personality, but that isn't a crime. If you get to know her she has a kind heart,' Ah Lan defended Jade.

Jade was aware of her opponents and made sure no one could complain about her work attitude. She was unfazed when she was assigned to labour on the farm and worked as hard as anyone else on the commune[18]. Privately, she felt injustice.

'My father was an important man and he loved me dearly when he was alive. I had servants to take care of my every need,' said Jade who had elitist notions even though she claimed to be a true Communist. 'I was the pearl in his palm.'

Jade had a wicked tongue and Ah Lan knew better than to contradict her. Her mother-in-law told her that Jade craved Wong's attention but it was Phoenix who was Wong's favourite child. She didn't mind Jade treating her like a maid but couldn't tolerate her criticism of Phoenix.

'Phoenix was a disappointment to my parents, she left them in a lurch at the first sign of trouble. My poor mother had no one to take care of her.'

'She had her own family to take care of. Mother-in-law was given a choice and she didn't want to go to Hong Kong.'

'What rubbish! Phoenix is a selfish daughter and mother. She wouldn't have burdened my mother with her daughter if she was so wonderful.'

Ah Lan let Jade have the last word. There was no winning this argument.

Jade was excited to hear that the government was restoring private houses to their pre-1949 owners. She felt the house belonged to her and that she was the rightful mistress, but unfortunately couldn't lay claim to it. Her late father Wong had given the deeds to Choy when he died.

In his darkest hour, Choy found God. He accepted Christianity through prison fellowship, which gave him hope after Pearl left him. The prison chaplain invited him to stay at the halfway house when he left prison.

'Brother Choy, you can choose a new beginning. We can offer

---

[18] During the Cultural Revolution, everyone was paid the same so there was no incentive to work hard.

you a room and board at our halfway house and work with employers who are willing to hire ex-prisoners.'

'Thank you, Chaplain. I'm tired of the life in the Triad. I don't want to end up in the prison again, I think I have a better chance of surviving in China. I heard that the government is returning confiscated properties to their rightful owners. I am penniless here in Hong Kong but if I can take back my ancestral house, I can make a decent living from collecting rent.'

'I will see if you we can find a sponsor to send you home, if it will help set you on the right path.'

A battle of wills began when Choy returned to find that Jade claimed to be the rightful owner of their ancestral house. Although he had lost the deed, the local authorities gave him a chance to search the archives to find a copy. The family feud provided interesting fodder for village gossip.

Villagers were split in their allegiance. Many women supported Jade in her bid as Choy, with his tattoos and rough mannerisms, looked threatening. The older men didn't care about whether Choy was a gangster, they simply didn't want to set a precedent in the village that allowed women to have property rights.

'Second Sister, I'm happy to let you live here as long as you like but the house belongs to me. I am the only son. Why are you fighting over the ownership?'

'We live in a new world. Inheritance doesn't pass through from father to son. Big Sister has forfeited her share by running away so the house should belong to me, since I am the next in line.'

It enraged Jade even further when the local authorities told her that Uncle Liu's adopted son Bing had made his claim on the house too. A shouting match ensued when she bumped into him at the administrative review office.

'You're a thief! The house belongs to the Wongs not the Lius – give me the deeds!'

'Your brother sold it to my father. You should blame your brother for giving up the house!' Bing downplayed the fact that his father was a human trafficker during the Cultural Revolution and helped to smuggle people like Choy out of China.

This was a shocking revelation to Jade. All this while, she thought Choy had lost the deeds.

'It's a disgrace that you sold it to an outsider,' Jade berated Choy.

Choy knew he had no ground to stand on. He had handed the deeds to Uncle Liu as collateral for his safe passage to Hong Kong.

'I admit it's my fault. We shouldn't be fighting each other, otherwise we risk losing the house to Bing.'

Thankfully for Jade and Choy, there was no proof that Choy had sold the house to Uncle Liu. The deeds were still in their father's name. The village custodian verified that their father was indeed deceased and the house belonged to his descendants – Jade and Choy.

It was a happy compromise for the pair. Choy felt it was un-Christian to squabble with his sister over worldly possessions. Jade gained a sense of pride to be the first female to own her own house in the village.

Jade didn't really want to fight with her brother; she was tired of being angry all the time. On the other hand, there was nothing to be happy about. She couldn't even pick on Ah Lan like she used to.

She didn't appreciate Choy trying to preach to her. It was a lost cause. She wasn't interested in any religion; although thankful the nuns saved her during the war, she had no faith that God had anything good planned for her.

Ah Lan was thankful to the Wong ancestors for a reunion with her husband. She was a simple woman who believed her place was by his side. She was contented with her life, having a shelter

159

over her head and food on her table, praying only for the safety of her husband.

Now that he was back, she didn't know how to behave around him. It was awkward to share a bed with a stranger but she was relieved to find he didn't expect her to perform any wifely duties. They lived like brother and sister.

She was a nurse to Choy as his health deteriorated.

When he died, Jade had no qualms about taking over Choy's share of the property. After all, Choy and Ah Lan had no children ... Who would they leave the money to anyway? Ah Lan avoided confrontation with Jade by moving to the ancestral hall.

She was getting too old to be at Jade's beck and call. She sought a quiet life taking care of the ancestors.

That was where June found her.

11

Finding Roots

June didn't have high hopes when she travelled to China in search of her grandmother's gold bracelet. She made the journey because she wanted to find out more about her beloved grandmother and her home country, but she had no idea what to expect.

At her father's request, his cousin agreed to be her tour guide. As June cleared customs at Hong Kong airport, she looked into the sea of faces for her cousin-uncle. All she had was a photo of a man with a moptop, wearing big shades and bellbottom trousers.

'Ka Bao! Over here!' Much to her relief, the man who called out her name no longer looked like a member of The Beatles. She immediately saw the family resemblance between her father and his cousin. The high forehead and long earlobes that were supposed to be a sign of good luck clearly ran in the family.

'How are you, Uncle Sum? Thank you for picking me up.'

'No problem – we are all family. This is your Aunty Sum. The last time we saw you in Singapore, you were still a little baby!'

'Hello, Aunty Sum. I brought you barbecue sliced pork from Singapore. Hope you like it!'

'Thank you, Ka Bao. You are so thoughtful but you didn't have to get us anything. We are happy to have a young person stay with us. It has been so long since …'

Her father had warned her that her cousin-aunty would get

emotional about her son. They had immigrated to Canada and put him in boarding school. He died in a car crash while his parents were visiting Hong Kong.

'It's just a small token of my appreciation. I'm looking forward to my stay.'

'Let's go home. I'm sure you would like a bath and a proper meal after your flight,' Uncle Sum said as he took her luggage from her. Even his mannerisms reminded her of her father.

That night at dinner, June asked Uncle Sum about their relations. She found it hard to remember who was related to whom and how.

'Your father and I have a common ancestor. Our fathers were cousins – we were born in the same village and like your father, I moved to Hong Kong when I was very young. My grandmother still lives in our ancestral village. She remembers when your father was born.'

'She must be very old.'

'She keeps her mind active by playing mahjong. We told her about your visit – she's very eager to see you!'

'And I can't wait to meet her.'

June was very excited on the ferry journey to China; she was going to visit the village where both her father and grandfather were born. Her grandmother didn't talk about her husband, June's grandfather; June had few memories of him as he died when she was very young.

She remembered Buddhist monks chanting prayers at his wake, alongside relatives playing mahjong until the wee hours of the morning. It was noisy enough to wake the dead. She was frightened by stories from her cousins about dead people coming back to life if a pregnant cat walked under the coffin. She didn't dare to look at her grandfather in the open casket when told to pay her last respects.

'You're very quiet,' said Uncle Sum.

'I can't believe I'm finally here, where it all began.'

'I'm glad you're so interested in your roots. All Chinese should be proud of who they are and where they came from.'

'My grandmother used to tell me stories of her childhood in China – good stories. I know a lot has happened since then and I may be only seeing one side of the coin.'

'It's not black and white. For years, my mother and I were separated. I thought of her constantly. I sent money to the village in the hope our relatives would take care of her. When I first went back to China, I was worried the authorities would imprison me for leaving without permission in the first place. Some of our friends and relatives didn't want to meet me for fear of implicating themselves. With the reunification, the main-landers are warming up to us Hong Kongers and vice versa.'

'I hope that means a warm reception for us!'

'Of course, you'll be welcomed with open arms. We're almost there.'

June was amused by the welcome party that greeted them as they arrived. Children waving flags and flowers shouted, 'Welcome, welcome, you are warmly welcome!' She then found out that they were there for their foreign exchange teacher, who was on the same ferry.

'So what did you think about the warm reception?' joked Uncle Sum.

'It was beyond my expectations. I am impressed!' June laughed.

There was a sea of humanity at the terminal, all hawking their services. Some gave out flyers for hotels, restaurants and tours while others sold food and drinks.

There was a welcome party of one for June and her uncle; their driver Ah Ming. Uncle Sum had hired him on his past trips to the village.

'Ah Ming is a reliable and safe driver. He used to be from our village but moved to the city to make money,' Uncle Sum told June as Ah Ming carted their luggage to the car.

'I've never seen so many motorcycles!' June was overwhelmed as the car drove out onto the main road. 'I expected more bicycles.'

'That was the iconic image of China when the doors were first opened to the outside world, but now everyone wants to own a motorcycle. Especially those with overseas Chinese relatives who can afford to buy imported goods with foreign currency. However it's far more comfortable to travel to the countryside on four wheels rather than two; the roads to the villages are still underdeveloped. Trust me when I say you don't want to be riding on a motorcycle on dirt roads. Your bum will be screaming for help!'

June laughed. Her Uncle Sum was unexpectedly candid in his description.

June watched the world go by through the windows of the car as she hummed to Cantonese pop music on the radio. Guangzhou, what used to be called Canton, was close enough to Hong Kong to be able to pick up the radio stations.

June enjoyed the change of scenery as they travelled into the countryside. As they drove further away from the city, the radio was tuned in to the local stations that played folk songs in Mandarin about the beauty of China.

The only countryside that June had experienced before China was in Malaysia. She was used to road trips with her parents from Singapore to the capital city of Kuala Lumpur, along highways that were flanked by rubber plantations on both sides.

When Ah Ming found out that she was from Singapore and it was her first time to China, he took the opportunity to show off the city. He gave a running commentary of everything they came across on the road. It was great, except that he had a habit of turning around to talk to her instead of watching the traffic.

Uncle Sum sat up front with Ah Ming and seemed oblivious to his reckless driving. He snored loudly as he nodded off. June prayed to her grandmother's spirit to take them safely to the village.

June's heart raced each time they drove close to a village. She would ask, 'Are we there yet?', Ah Ming would reply 'No' and she would look longingly out of the window for the next village to appear.

'Do you see that house over there? When the Japanese invaded, many of villagers, including my grandfather, were captured and shot there. It is rumoured to be very haunted by angry spirits. A child recently fell into the outhouse and died.' Ah Ming pointed out a hut in the middle of a field as he narrowly missed running over a buffalo on the side of the road.

'We're almost there.' Uncle Sum suddenly woke up, right on cue.

The village was no different from the ones they had passed along the way. It was a collection of houses with a temple and a school surrounded by open fields but to June, this village was special. It held the key to the mystery of her grandmother's bracelet.

Friends and family were gathered at Great-grandaunt Sum's house. They had heard about June's visit and wanted to meet the young relative from Singapore. The population of the village was aged, as young people moved out to work in the cities and left their grandparents and parents to tend to the farms.

Land and labour were cheaper in the countryside and there was a trend to build factories that were now slowly replacing the farmland. The young people who moved in were immigrants from inland regions of China, who often didn't speak Cantonese and didn't mix with the locals.

Great-grandaunt Sum and her friends chatted about the good old days when the village kinship was strong; children lived close to their parents and took care of them in old age. It was a treat to have a young girl like June who was interested in tracing her roots.

Before June even walked into the house, Great-grandaunt Sum picked out her voice and greeted her at the door.

'There you are! I have been so looking forward to your visit that my neck is longer than a giraffe's.' Great-grandaunt Sum was a sprightly centenarian who tottered around quickly, despite her tiny bound feet. Her thinning white hair was pulled back neatly in a bun. When she smiled, the sunlight bounced off the gold caps on her front teeth.

June smiled and thought, 'I know where Uncle Sum got his sense of humour from.'

'I'm sorry to keep you waiting so long. I am happy to see everyone!'

'Now that you are here, you will have to stay at least until dinner so we can have a good chat. Let me introduce you to all your uncles and aunties.'

Great-grandaunt Sum immediately rattled off the names of the relatives and friends who were gathered in her house, even though June had a hard time keeping track of who was who. Some of these distant relatives were more closely related to their driver Ah Ming than to her. Nonetheless, June was respectful and addressed each one by their family titles.

'Don't worry if you don't remember who we are. You can dispense with formality and just call me Aunty. I want to stay young!' said one of the elderly women in the group.

Great-grandaunt Sum passed around the barbecue sliced pork that June brought for everyone to snack on.

'I feel like I'm celebrating New Year!' said June.

'Well, it is a family reunion, just like New Year,' said Great-grandaunt Sum as she patted her head lovingly. 'It would be great if your father and mother could come with you next time. I know this is a special trip for you. Your uncle said you have many questions for me.'

'Can you tell me more about my grandfather and grandmother? What were they like when they were young?'

'Has your father not told you the family stories?'

'No, he doesn't like to talk about his life in China very much. He says he was too little to remember and when he was older, he was too busy working to listen to his mother's stories about their homeland.'

'Well, where shall we begin? I suppose we should start with how we are related. Your great-grandfather was my husband's brother. The reason we don't share the same surname is because my husband married into our family[19]. Elder Cheng, your great-grandfather, was a close friend of the Wongs. It was no surprise that your grandfather Long married the Wong's eldest daughter, Phoenix.

'I remember it was a lavish wedding. Your great-grandfather was a retired civil servant and spared no expense to celebrate the union of the two families. From what I heard, your grandmother Phoenix was a good wife. She was submissive and obedient to her husband as women were expected to be. The role of women has changed a lot since the Communist Revolution.

'Just like everyone else, your family experienced some tough times during the war. Your great-grandparents died during a plague – the same one that killed my husband. Rumour has it that your great-grandfather had several mistresses who ganged up to blackmail your grandfather. They threatened to make a scene at the funeral if he didn't give up a share of the estate to his half brothers. Your grandfather continued to work as a respected but underpaid teacher until the war broke out. Your grandparents had two children – a son and a daughter.'

'I didn't know I had an aunty!' June was shocked by this revelation.

'Your grandmother may not have talked about her because she died a tragic death. Your grandparents escaped to Hong Kong with your father during the Communist Revolution, while your aunty stayed behind with Mei – not her grandmother by

---

[19] It was not uncommon for Chinese men to be adopted as a husband into an influential family if there was no male heir. The husband and the subsequent offspring would take on the wife's family name.

blood but the second wife of her grandfather, so her grand-mother in all other respects. I have heard different accounts of how she died, but no one really knows what happened. All I know is that she was kidnapped and probably died when she tried to escape. Your grandmother's mother died not long after.'

'My grandmother must have been devastated.'

'Any parent would be. When my first son died, I lost my will to live. I stopped eating for days. No parent should have to bury their children. I wanted to throw myself into the ground with my boy but I had to live on for my other children. I think your grandmother did the same. She had to be strong for your father.'

'I didn't know she went through so much. She never mentioned anything about her daughter – it was as though she never existed.'

'Denial could be the only way she could deal with the pain.'

'Do you know if I have any other relatives living here?'

'The descendants of your grandfather's half brothers still live around here, if you want to meet them. I don't know your grandmother's family as well – she had a brother and a sister but I don't know if they're still alive. You can visit her hometown and check the ancestral temple for records of your extended family, but bear in mind many of these records were destroyed during the Communist Revolution.'

'When my grandmother died, she left me this pawn ticket. Can you make any sense of this?' 'Unfortunately I don't recognise the name of the pawn shop.' Great-grandaunt Sum squinted at the yellowing piece of paper through her glasses. 'What's odd is that it's dated before the war. During the Japanese invasion there was a food shortage. You had to pay through the nose to buy anything on the black market. Many people had to sell or pawn their valuables to survive but it seems your grandmother had financial difficulties even before the war. Since the description of the item is a dragon phoenix bracelet, it is possible that she pawned off a piece of her bridal dowry. Women usually held their bridal dowry close to their hearts, as it was often the only thing of value they could call their own. It was only sold at a last resort.'

'I wonder what would have prompted my grandmother to do that? I didn't expect to find more mysteries!'

'Maybe the people in your grandmother's village will recognise the name of the shop. When we go there to find your relatives, we could ask around about this pawn shop and see what we can find out,' Uncle Sum chimed in.

'Thank you for going to all this trouble.'

'Don't worry, I'm happy to help! You are family, after all. And it's not every day that I get to play detective. I feel like Charlie Chan, solving mysteries.'

'I don't know Charlie Chan. Is he related to Jackie Chan?'

'Aiyah! That's a sign of our generation gap. Charlie Chan is an American Chinese detective, not related in any way to the Hong Kong actor Jackie Chan!'

June was overwhelmed by the number of people who turned up for the village feast, all courtesy of her father. Short tables were set up outside Great-grandaunt Sum's house while relatives and neighbours supplied their own wooden stools. They gathered around the shade of the big banyan tree and caught up on the latest gossip. June was sure they were sizing her up as a potential wife for their grandsons.

'While we wait for dinner to start, take June to the ancestral temple to make an offering,' Great-grandaunt Sum said to Uncle Sum before taking off to supervise the caterers.

'You heard your great-grandaunt. Let's go and burn some joss sticks for our ancestors.'

June expected to see a grand building decorated with glazed porcelain tiles and mystical beasts on the roofs, like the temples in Chinatown. The ancestral temple turned out to be a modest building that looked no different from a village hall.

'Here is where we house the village patron gods and the ancestral tablets. The original temple was damaged during the

169

war and the Cultural Revolution. Although the villagers were able to raise enough money to rebuild the temple, it's a far cry from its former glory.'

Inside the temple, coils of incense gave off a cloying sweet fragrance as the wisps of smoke ascended to the heavens above.

'Wow, it's so hot in here! It feels like I just stepped into a sauna,' June exclaimed as she looked around the temple.

June didn't have to look far to find evidence of her family history. On one wall was the Cheng family tree, going back to the twelfth century.

'I think I see my grandfather's name on this tablet, but not my father's.'

'People do get left out of the family tree, especially if they've gone abroad. Once it's carved, the tablet doesn't get updated regularly. Surprisingly, the further back you go in the family line, the more accurate the information. Villagers were less mobile in the old days. Many lived and died in the same village as their forefathers.'

The temple custodian came to greet them. 'What Ah Sum said is absolutely true. We do try our best to get information from our overseas villagers. I am the custodian here and may be able to help you trace your history.'

'Ah ... Second Uncle. It's good to see you. This is Cheng Kyong's daughter.'

'Hello, Grand-uncle. My name is Cheng Ka Bao; my English name is June. I'm visiting from Singapore,' June politely explained to the old man. She figured if this man was Uncle Sum's uncle, than he would be her grand-uncle.

'I was looking forward to meeting you at the village feast. I'm glad you dropped by. I'm sorry your father was left out of the tablet – it was an oversight, which we'll correct in the new tablet. Times have changed. With the one child policy, people are not having as many male descendants as they did in the past. We should really include the names of our female descendants and that means you will be included on the new tablet. Do give me your address before you leave. I'll write to your father and see if he's willing to contribute to the temple funds that will go into such projects.'

'Oh, I see. OK, I suppose so.' June was caught by surprise by the request for money.

Uncle Sum came to the rescue. 'I'll make a small donation on our behalf for the joss sticks.'

'Thanks, Uncle Sum. I'll pray for ...'

'Don't tell me. Otherwise it won't come true!' Uncle Sum interrupted her before she could finish.

When June got back to Great-grandaunt Sum's, the ten-course dinner was just about to start. She was not the only hungry guest looking forward to a feast.

'I'm being eaten alive – I've never seen so many mosquitoes in my life!' June tried hard to keep her composure and not scratch.

'The village is surrounded by rice paddies, an excellent breeding ground for mosquitoes. In the past, farmers would rear larvae-eating fish but many of the farms that have been sold to build factories are lying unused. Mosquito control is becoming more of a problem.' Uncle Sum looked genuinely concerned, but was soon back to usual self.

'Even though Cantonese are known to eat "anything with four legs except a table and anything that flies except an aeroplane", we haven't managed to conquer the mosquito!'

'I seem to be the only one covered in bites,' observed June. 'Everyone else must be immune to them.'

'You are young and tender. We are all old and weathered like the water buffaloes. Not even the mosquitoes are interested in us!' Great-grandaunt Sum chuckled. 'I'll get someone to light a mosquito coil under the table to keep the bugs away from your juicy flesh.'

Although June was enjoying her time with Great-grandaunt Sum in the village, she was secretly relieved that she was going to spend the night at a hotel in town.

*   *   *

It was another long drive the following day. In the car, Uncle Sum and Ah Ming were subdued, hungover from the celebrations of the night before.

Her grandmother's village was not very different from the one she had just visited. What stood out was an ornate village gate. The Corinthian columns, with a faux-marble finish, stood in stark contrast to the traditional village homes.

'That's an odd-looking piece of architecture,' June remarked.

'A newly minted villager must have paid for that monstrosity,' said Uncle Sum.

'In the old days, the emperor would build archways for people as a sign of their loyalty and contribution to the country,' added Ah Ming. 'Nowadays, rich overseas villagers can have their names forever etched in stone when they send money home for village projects.'

'Now that we're here, let's not waste time on our mission. Our first stop is the council offices, where they keep village archives.'

When they arrived, Uncle Sum introduced himself to the village official. 'Hello, I am Albert Sum. This young lady's grandmother is from this village. She wants to check to see if there are any living relatives.'

'It's great to see young people like you interested in your heritage. Can you give me your name and your grandmother's name? Do you have her date of birth?'

'My name is Cheng Ka Bao. My grandmother's name is Phoenix Wong. I'm embarrassed to say I don't remember her date of birth but she was born in the year of the Rabbit. She left China with my grandfather Cheng Long shortly after the Japanese war.'

'I'll take a look at our records. I may be able to give you some information if you come back tomorrow.'

'Actually, I don't have much time in China. I was hoping to

just spend the day here. Is there any way you can speed up the process?'

'It'll take time to go through the written records. You could talk to the Wong ancestral temple custodian – he's one of the oldest villagers and knows all about local history. He may remember your grandmother and her family. The Wong ancestral temple is at the end of the village. You can come back here later if you still need my help.'

'I expected the council official to know everything about the village,' said June to Uncle Sum, after they had thanked him and taken their leave.

'The council officials may not have originally come from this village. During the days of the Cultural Revolution, urban youths were sent to rural villages for re-education. Don't worry, it's not the end of the road. The temple custodian may be able to point us in the right direction.'

Along the way, they walked passed numerous old houses. One in particular caught her attention. It had a large courtyard in the middle, where clothes and vegetables had been left to dry in the sun. The doorway of the house had 'Wong' written on it.

'Do you think this could be my great-grandfather's house?'

'It's hard to say. Anyone in this village could have the same surname as your grandmother.'

At the temple, June found the custodian was also a Wong.

'I do know your grandmother; we're distant cousins. Your grandmother had a half brother and a half sister. You don't need to look any further for your grand-uncle's wife – she's right here!'

'Ah Lan, you have a visitor!' he called to someone in the backroom. 'Ah Lan is very devout and has a heart of gold. She protected the statue of Guan Gong from the Red Guards during the Cultural Revolution. She is our most active volunteer.'

A little old lady appeared. She had a short bob that looked like she cut it herself. Her face was tanned and weathered, like a labourer.

'Hello, Grand-aunt. I am Ka Bao, Phoenix's granddaughter.'

'Oh dear – I never thought this day would come!' Ah Lan hugged June and broke down in tears.

Despite Ah Lan's heavy local accent, June understood that she was happy to see her.

'Our ancestors have answered my prayers – I hoped to see my family before I died. You look just like your grandmother. Is she here?'

'My grandmother just passed away. I'm making this journey in memory of her. I think she has an unfulfilled wish; she left me this pawn ticket in her will.' June held back tears thinking about her grandmother.

'It's no wonder she never wrote back to me. She was a good person and will receive blessings in her afterlife. I'm so happy you found your way to me … I was the one who sent this pawn ticket to your grandmother when my husband died. I was hoping to make amends.'

This was the moment June was waiting for; the moment of truth.

'Your grandmother was not the one who pawned the gold bracelet. It was my husband, your grand-uncle, Choy, who did so without her knowledge. Your grand-aunt, Jade, was in need of money to save her adopted daughter, who was kidnapped. When your grandmother found out, she requested your grand-uncle to pass the bracelet to Jade. Instead of doing so, he pawned the bracelet and took the money.

'It's been a great source of regret that I couldn't stop his actions. He was a selfish man and did many terrible things – but he was my husband and it was my place to stand by his side. He too was in Hong Kong but never looked up your grandmother for fear of revealing his misdeeds. Choy fell into bad company and was involved in the Triad. He became a sick man in his old age and returned here to ask for my forgiveness and help. Your great-grandmother treated me like her own daughter. I had to fulfill my duty as his wife to take care of him. Many times I tried

174

to persuade him to contact your grandmother but he refused. On his deathbed, Choy had a change of heart. He took out the pawn ticket that he had kept all those years and asked me to post it to your grandmother with a note to say he was sorry. I wondered if your grandmother would understand when she received the pawn ticket … There is someone else I think you should meet.'

June was surprised when Ah Lan led her to the house with the courtyard that she had noticed earlier.

'Is this my great-grandfather's house?'

'Yes, this used to be my father-in-law's house before they lost their fortune. The house was annexed during the Cultural Revolution and subdivided into small apartments to house several families. Your great-grandfather was a wealthy man. This house was passed down many generations of Wongs – it was a great disappointment to my mother-in-law that we lost everything.

'The house was returned to Jade and Choy when the government restored confiscated properties to their original owners. Since your grand-uncle died, only your grand-aunt lives here with the tenants …'

Before Ah Lan could continue, she heard a woman's voice shout, 'Ah Lan, is that you? Why are you skulking around? Are you trying to steal from me?'

'Don't worry. That's your grand-aunt Jade. She's a bit unstable but I think she would be happy to find out that you're here. One thing you have to know is that Jade bore a grudge against your grandmother for not helping her. I hope you can make things right.'

June didn't know if she was ready for such a big responsibility.

12

Family Reunion

'June, I can guess what's going through your mind. You just want to find the gold bracelet and go home. I know it's asking a lot of you to be the peacemaker for your grandmother and her sister – you don't have to do it if you don't want to.'

June was amazed that Ah Lan read her so well.

'I think my grandmother wanted me to make this journey. I'll do my best to see it through to the end.'

'Your grandmother was probably unaware of her sister's bad feelings towards her.'

'Why do you think it would make a difference if I went to Grand-aunt Jade?'

'You can tell her that your grandmother wanted to help her. The pawn ticket is proof that she gave up her gold bracelet. Beyond her hard exterior, she's a lonely woman who needs love. She may have given up on your grandmother but they were sisters, after all. You can restore that love by telling her the truth.'

'It would mean more if I could find the gold bracelet; that would be the perfect peace offering.'

'That may be easier said than done. Choy pawned the bracelet to a man called Fung, who is now dead. His family's pawn shop was destroyed during the war but he still has family living in this village. You could visit them to find out if they remember anything about it.'

June and Uncle Sum set off to visit Fung's family.

'Hello, I'm Ah Lan's grand-niece, Ka Bao. She told me that my grand-uncle pawned an item at your family's shop. This is the ticket. It would really mean a lot to us if we could find it again,' June explained to the lady who answered the door.

'Well, this is a surprise. I am Fung Gui Ying. The pawn shop belonged to my grandfather – I haven't heard anyone talk about it for a very long time. Do come in, we can chat over a cup of tea.'

'Thank you! This means so much to me.'

'You know, I may not be of much help. Our pawn shop was bombed during the Japanese invasion; we were fortunate to escape with our lives,' Miss Fung told June as she offered her tea.

'Sounds terrible.' June felt genuinely fortunate that she had not had to go through such traumatic wartime experiences.

'Yes, it was bad. My grandfather was devastated when the shop burnt down. He said that every item in the shop had a rightful owner and he felt responsible for the safekeeping of these valuables until their owners could claim them back. He tried to put out the fire – he was hurt and would have been burnt alive if my grandmother and my father hadn't pulled him to safety. After the war, there were people who suspected that we were the ones who set fire to our shop. We would never do anything like that! What happened during the war was a travesty – just like everyone else, we lost all we had. It took years for us to rebuild our lives again.'

'I admire your grandfather for his brave efforts. It must have been hard for him to deal with the accusations. I'm sure if my grandmother were still alive, she wouldn't blame him for the loss of her gold bracelet. The bracelet was pawned without her knowledge and since the person to blame is now long dead, there's no one to hold a grudge against.'

'Do you have the pawn ticket for this gold bracelet?'

'Sure.' June handed over the ticket.

Miss Fung gasped as she read the description. 'What you're looking for is a dragon phoenix gold bracelet?'

'Have you seen it?' June asked.

'Yes, I have.' Miss Fung rolled up her long sleeve to reveal a gold bracelet on her wrist. 'I believe this is what you are looking for! It was the only item to survive the fire. My grandfather had to wait days to get permission to return to the shop to salvage what was left. Looters stole whatever wasn't destroyed. All that remained was a charred, smoking shell. My grandfather was so upset that he fell to his knees and wept – it was then he saw a glint of gold among the ashes, which turned out to be this bracelet. The looters may have overlooked it or dropped it in their haste to get away. My grandfather told my grandmother it was a sign from the heavens not to give up; from the ashes, the phoenix will rise. There's an inscription on the inside that kept our family going through the hard times.' Miss Fung removed the bracelet and handed it over to June.

June read the inscription aloud, 'A family in harmony will prosper in everything'.

'My grandfather couldn't get treatment for his burns so although they weren't life-threatening to start with, infection set in and eventually killed him. Because of our tainted family background, my father was assigned to janitorial work while my uncle was sent to dig ditches. Our family had to attend struggle sessions every day and barely scraped by with the food rations that they received. My brothers and sisters always shared what little we had. Our grandmother said our grandfather would not rest if peace if he knew we were fighting one another. She hid the bracelet under a roof tile so the Red Guards wouldn't find it when they ransacked the house. It was only after the Cultural Revolution that she dared to take it out again. No matter how badly she was in need of money, she didn't sell the bracelet. She felt that if she did, bad luck would befall the family. Before she died, she gave the bracelet to me, her oldest grandchild. She told me to promise never to sell it or pawn it.'

'Since the bracelet was never claimed, I know by rights it belongs to you. I hope you'll make a special concession and allow me buy it back.'

'Although my grandmother said never to sell or pawn the bracelet, she did say that I should return it to its rightful owner if I ever had the chance. Since your grandmother gave you the ticket, this bracelet should belong to you.'

June was surprised at Miss Fung's act of kindness. 'Thank you! Thank you for fulfilling my grandmother's wishes.' She closed her eyes and held the bracelet tightly in her palm as though if she squeezed it hard enough, she would travel through time and space to her grandmother.

'I miss her so much!' said June as tears rolled down her cheeks.

'I miss my grandmother too,' said Miss Fung. 'It's strange how the bracelet brought our families together. Maybe our grandmothers have become friends in the afterlife.'

'Thanks to your generosity, the bracelet can help me resolve a family feud on my grandmother's behalf.'

With the bracelet in hand, June set off to meet Jade. She knew the meeting with her grand-aunt wasn't going to be easy. After all, Jade held a deep grudge against her grandmother. She was thankful that Ah Lan was by her side.

It was the first time she got to see her ancestral home up close. The paint had chipped away in many places but she could still see some of the intricate carvings on the walls and pillars. Ah Lan was telling her how grand the house had looked in the past when she heard a woman's voice.

'Ah Lan, is that you again? Why are you snooping around here? I told you to stay away!' A grumpy-looking old woman walked out from one of the main rooms.

'Big Sister, don't get angry. We have a special guest – I wanted her to meet you.' Ah Lan worked quickly to appease Jade.

'Who's this, then?' Jade looked at June.

179

'This is our grand-niece Ka Bao, Phoenix's granddaughter.'

'How are you, Grand-aunt?' June said to Jade.

'Unless Choy had a bastard child, I cannot possibly have any grand-nieces or grand-nephews.' Jade ignored June and spoke to Ah Lan like she wasn't there.

'Please be rational. You can't deny that Phoenix is your sister. I know there is some misunderstanding – Ka Bao is here to clear that up. Let's sit down and talk.'

'Fine, I will give you one minute of my time. After all, I have nothing else better to do.'

Ah Lan gave June a reassuring smile and urged her to follow Jade.

'Grand-aunt, I have something that belongs to you.' June presented Jade with a jewelry box.

'What's this?' Jade was curious and opened the box. 'I don't understand ... I've never seen this bracelet before.'

'Many years ago, my grandmother entrusted Grand-uncle Choy to pass you this bracelet when you had difficulties. It never made its way to you. When my grandmother passed away she left me a pawn ticket for the bracelet, which I redeemed with the help of Grand-aunt Ah Lan and other goodhearted people. Although many things have changed, I hope you will accept my grandmother's gift of love.'

'So what Ah Lan said was true!' Jade was stunned.

'I've been trying to tell you about this ever since Choy died!' said Ah Lan. 'He didn't want you to be angry with him while he was alive.'

'So I could have raised enough money to save my daughter during the war ... Why didn't your grandmother make that decision sooner and give me the bracelet when I asked her for help?'

'Phoenix did want you to have the bracelet, but Choy pawned it,' Ah Lan interjected.

'Grand-aunt, that's all in the past. I hope the bracelet can bring you some peace of mind in the knowledge that my grandmother was ready to help you. Whenever I asked my grandmother about China, she spoke fondly of you.'

'You think you can wash away history by turning up one day with a present? You are too young and naïve!' Jade had held a grudge against her sister for too long to accept a different reality.

'Perhaps we should give you a chance to digest the news and come again next time,' Ah Lan stepped in. She didn't want June to bare the brunt of Jade's ranting.

'You'd better not take away the bracelet if you say that it's mine,' Jade said in response.

'That's not how I imagined my reunion with Grand-aunt Jade to turn out,' said a disappointed June to Ah Lan.

'I'm sorry I put you in such an awkward position. I am afraid Sister Jade is set in her ways. She's not willing to let go of the past.' Ah Lan shook her head.

'You don't need to apologize. I think my grandmother is proud of me for seeing this through to the end. At least the bracelet is now with Grand-aunt Jade, where it belongs.' June gave Ah Lan a hug.

Before June left China, she asked Ah Lan if there was any way she could help her.

'Don't worry about me. I can manage just fine. The government gives me social welfare because I am a childless elderly.'

'I know you're very capable. All the same, I would like to see you again and write to you so you won't forget about me.'

Ah Lan laughed whole-heartedly. 'I'm not senile – at least not yet! How can I forget about you? I would be happy if you wrote to me once in a while.'

Although June still grieved for her grandmother's passing, she felt comforted that it was through her death she met Grand-aunt Ah Lan. When one door closed, another one opened.

One month after she returned to Singapore, June received a letter from Japan in beautiful Chinese script.

'Dad, can you read this letter?' June was very excited. 'The handwriting is so cursive I find it hard to read. I think it may be from a relative.'

'How can you be Chinese and not be able to read Chinese? Your trip to China hasn't taught you anything!' Kyong replied.

'I don't need another lecture about my Chinese. Aren't you happy that you're still useful for something?' June teased her father.

Kyong put on his reading glasses and read the letter. Occasionally, he smiled and sighed as June waited eagerly.

'Come on, Dad – the letter's for me! Are you going to tell me what it says?'

'This letter is from my long-lost cousin. She was reunited recently with your grand-aunt Jade, who told her all about you. It turns out that a kind Japanese couple intervened when she was going to be sold as a slave. They treated her like a daughter and took her to Japan to escape the war. She was given a Japanese education and eventually married a Japanese/Chinese man. Through all those years, she never forgot her adopted mother who loved and cared for her. She promised that when both her Japanese adopted parents passed away, she would make a trip to China to find your grand-aunt. When she appeared, your grand-aunt was so elated that she couldn't stop laughing and crying. She also met Ah Lan. Apparently, your two grand-aunties made peace after your trip. She said that Jade wants to tell you that she was happy that you visited her and that you brought good luck. She wants you to have the gold bracelet and will hold on to it for safekeeping.'

'You know, Dad, I think it's time that you visited China.'

'Whatever you say, my dear daughter,' Kyong smiled.